MEN DON'T CRY

This book has been selected to receive financial assistance from English PEN's 'PEN Translates' programme, supported by Arts Council England. English PEN exists to promote literature and our understanding of it, to uphold writers' freedoms around the world, to campaign against the persecution and imprisonment of writers for stating their views, and to promote the friendly co-operation of writers and the free exchange of ideas. www.englishpen.org

MEN DON'T CRY

Faïza Guène

translated by Sarah Ardizzone

Abuja - London

This edition first published in 2021 by Cassava Republic Press

Abuja - London

A CIP catalogue record for this book is available from the National Library of Nigeria and the British Library.

ISBN 978-1-911115-69-4
eISBN 978-1-911115-70-0

Book design by Tobi Ajiboye
Cover design by Jamie Keenan
Printed and bound in Great Britain by Bell and Bain Ltd., Glasgow

Distributed worldwide by Ingram Publishers Services

In memory of my father.

In memory of Isabelle Seguin.

It Might Come in Handy

As in all my childhood memories, there was food on the table. Lots of food. And my mother was complaining about the weather being too hot. Or too cold. The point being she was complaining.

It was the day Big Baba had decided to install that stupid satellite dish. My father looked so pleased with himself when the first Arabic channel popped up on our screen. We watched a fat man with a moustache reading out the football results, while his belt sliced his paunch in two.

A new world beckoned. Dozens and dozens of channels paraded before our eyes: Morocco, Algeria, Tunisia, Egypt, Dubai, Yemen, Jordan, Qatar.... My mother was overcome with emotion. At last, Big Baba was giving her the honeymoon she'd always dreamed of.

No more cold sweats for me when the Tahiti Shower ad came on: 'Has anyone seen the remote?'

My mother blushing, her hands pressed to her cheeks: 'Yéééé h'chouma!'

My sister, Mina: 'Look what those feminists have won for us!'

My mother, in disgust: 'Tfffou, feminists!'

My sister Dounia: 'You're not going to bring that up again?!'

In the old days, after those kinds of heated conversations, we always switched off the television and sank into a depressing silence. But once our life turned towards a new satellite, my mother swore by the cookery programmes on Abu Dhabi TV, or the Turkish costume sagas dubbed into Moroccan dialect on 2M TV. The atmosphere at home became a touch more folkloric.

'Now that's what I call work!' pronounced Big Baba, whistling cheerily as he put his screwdrivers away in his toolbox.

He loved DIY; fixing things, salvaging.

Mainly salvaging.

Our garden had turned into a graveyard of scrap metal. Corroded old washing machines, corrugated iron, park benches, road signs, a tennis umpire's chair, a dozen typewriters, a restaurant sign, the headlights from a Citroën ZX, a giant freezer and two wooden horses, worn out from their carousel life.

How does he manage to transport all that junk? we wondered. But he found a way.

Each time he brought a new toy home, my mother's blood pressure shot up for several days. 'Ya Rabi! What are you going to do with *that*?!'

And each time, he gave the same ridiculous answer, 'It might come in handy, one day!'

He held that nothing should be thrown away. Would you expect any less of a retired cobbler?

'No, it won't, it will NEVER come in handy! Not today, not tomorrow, not ever! People threw it away because it *stopped being handy* – it's useless! My God! Why are you doing this to me? Bring me a glass of water! Quick! My heart! I'm having palpitations! A glass of water!'

My mother would wince, clutch her chest and down the

glass in one: her tragic actress turn.

Over the years, she had watched her dream French garden, with its symmetrical hedges and tidy vegetable patch, disappear beneath mounds of rusty objects. She was left with no choice but to sit in a chair, her arms dangling and a faraway look in her eyes, as she gazed at the printed fruit on the waxed tablecloth.

'35 years nailing soles onto shoes!' Big Baba used to say, when I was a kid. 'Bang, bang, bang! All my life, I wore out my hands so my children could work with their heads!'

Academic success meant everything in his eyes.

'Sit next to me and tell me what's written here before I sign it,' he would say, when we brought our school reports home.

One by one, I would recite my marks, along with the teacher's comments, proudly pointing out that there was no red pen in the behaviour column.

'Well done, my son. I'm pleased.'

Slowly, with a Bic biro, he would affix his miniscule signature; one that was shaky and feverish, betraying nothing of his robust character. Then, like a doctor, he would put the lid back on and clip his biro next to the others in his shirt pocket, even though he couldn't read or write.

For years we held a straight course: Big Baba steering his little troop calmly, just as when he was at the wheel of his 1983 Renault 11 Turbo.

Then came the first hairpin bends: Dounia, my eldest sister, had started growing up.

There are certain scenes that stick in my mind. Big Baba circling Dounia like a crime squad investigator in full interrogation mode, his hands behind his back.

'Where were you? Have you seen what time it is? I'll

teach you to show me respect. Do you think your name is Christine?'

I suspect my sister often wished she was called Christine.

Today, her name might as well be Christine.

Dounia

When she was a teenager, Dounia had a best friend: Julie Guérin. That was when the troubles began. Julie triggered the psychological process of my sister's 'Christine-isation'.

Julie was popular with all the boys at school; she was slim, wore designer clothes and kept a diary. Her parents sent her to summer camp in the Languedoc-Rousillon, near the border with Spain. Her mother let her go to night-time concerts and pin up posters of some American boy band in her bedroom. I don't remember the singers' names, but they were black and bare-chested.

Julie also had platform shoes, a boyfriend, a cat, a bedroom she didn't share with anybody else, and she even had permission to celebrate her birthday in her dad's garage.

In Dounia's eyes, Julie was living the dream. My sister was mesmerised, to the point that she was happy to play the friend in the shadows, the one who gets told, 'Hey! Look after my bag!'

It's worth pointing out that my sister's life was the exact opposite of Julie Guérin's.

In addition to her glasses, Dounia wore braces from the age of 15-18. She didn't know what to do with her long frizzy brown hair, so she braided it, twisted it in a thousand-and-one messy ways and piled it on top of her head. She hid her overweight body under baggy polo shirts and sweatpants. She wasn't allowed to go out, she shared her bedroom with my other sister, and as for posters, boyfriends, or holiday camps near Spain, let alone birthday celebrations in our dad's garage, forget it. Dounia's last resort was a diary, oh yes, because of course there was no danger of my father reading it.

Spending time with Julie made Dounia feel she was growing wings. She would say things like: 'At least Julie's allowed to...' and 'Julie's so lucky....' And then, one day:

'Maman, why don't you ever say, "I love you"? Julie's mum says it to her all the time.'

My mother was so taken aback she was briefly lost for words. Her big, brown khol-lined eyes bulged.

'What makes you ask that? You don't think we love you?'

Dounia rolled her eyes and shrugged. Then she took a swig of homemade citronnade straight from the bottle, which was guaranteed to infuriate my mother.

'And what about the glasses in the kitchen, are they just for decoration?'

'It's all right, okay, I haven't got AIDS.'

'Tfffou!'

Dounia was becoming insolent. And my mother, as usual, produced her weapon of personal mass destruction: the blame game.

Aim. Fire!

'Your grandfather was a revolutionary who fought in the war to liberate his country. A brave and courageous man. We were ten children fed on dry bread, who walked barefoot without complaining. You only have to look at all the sacrifices he made to raise us. Do you think we fretted about whether he loved us?'

'Whatever, Maman, I know that story of yours off by heart.

You weren't allowed to play outside. And he pulled you out of school at 13. So what kind of life is that, anyway? A horror movie?'

'That's got nothing to do with it! We were living in a different era. He took me out of school because he needed me to look after my brothers and sisters. He raised us to be good people!'

'D'you seriously think you raise your children to be good people by locking them up?'

'Nobody's locking *you* up!'

'Yes, they are! You never let me do anything. I'm not even allowed to wear jeans!'

'And that's why you're unhappy? Because we don't want you dressing like a cowboy?'

'It's called fashion! You don't understand. Take Julie's mum, she's got a young attitude, when she hangs out with her daughter, you'd think they were two friends...'

'Two *frrrriends*?'

My mother loves emphasising her astonishment; it's the dramatist in her.

'Do you think I had children to make myself some new friends? Tfffou! That's not being a mother. It's being afraid.'

'What I'm trying to say is, Julie's mum's modern. She works in an office and she drives a car.'

'Are you talking about Julie's mother or Julie's father, eh? Why would I follow the example of a woman who buys her daughter cigarettes? A woman who's killing her own child? And who borrows her trousers?'

'Why not? They're the same size...'

'Fine, so I'm fat. Where's the problem? I'm no fashion model. But let me tell you, when we were refugees in Morocco during the war, we used to dream at night of eating meat. We endured real hunger. Now I'm nice and plump, hamdoullah.'

'Julie's mum never asks her to cook or do the washing up. Anyone'd think it was the only thing that mattered in life.'

'Your sister, Mina, loves helping me in the kitchen, but you–'

'Here we go again! You're always comparing us...'

'What about when you get married, eh? You want me sending you to your husband's house having learnt nothing?'

'Who cares? I'll never get married, anyway.'

A butcher's knife plunged into my mother's gut would have had less effect. The stand-offs became increasingly frequent. Before that, we'd never heard any doors slam in our house. But there followed a period when they slammed so often that my father, fuming, took the girls' bedroom door off its hinges and hung up a curtain instead.

'Now try slamming the curtain!'

My mother even considered having Dounia exorcised. In the end, she banned her daughter from keeping company with Julie-harbinger-of-bad-luck, who caused her so much trouble.

'She's cursed, that girl. Cursed!'

After her parents' divorce, Julie tried to commit suicide and everyone in the neighbourhood felt sorry for her. With one notable exception.

My mother flaunted her mocking smile in full view of Dounia.

'You see! If your friend Julie's life was as wonderful as you claim, she wouldn't have wanted to die!'

Heavy silence, a hate-filled stare, followed by tossing of hair and, for the finishing touch, storming off to the bedroom with no door.

'You've got no heart, Maman. No heart.'

If there had been a door, Dounia would have slammed it, for sure. It was a scene worthy of the Mexican soaps dubbed into Arabic that my mother couldn't get enough of. To be honest, Dounia and Maman wiped the floor with those Latina drama queens...

In the years that followed, the situation with Dounia deteriorated. The outside world was full of Julie Guérins, and my parents tried in vain to keep their daughter in the nest. Threats and punishments didn't work any more. My mother, who was so cunning when it came to the blame game, had emptied all her cartridges. Her sudden palpitations and mounting blood pressure didn't change anything.

We had already lost Dounia.

As for Big Baba, he became resigned to this turn of events. He avoided confrontation and started behaving as if his daughter no longer existed, ignoring my mother's cries for help: 'Do something, Abdelkader!'

He took to mending the bicycles of local children in his shed at the bottom of the garden.

Dounia would return home later and later, with no explanation, letting on very little about her life. She almost never ate with us and kept to herself, her nose buried in her books. She studied hard, came first in all her subjects and, after leaving school with top grades in her baccalauréat exams, began studying Law as well as holding down a part-time job.

The transformation had begun. Within a few months, her curves had disappeared, along with her brace, she'd traded her pair of geeky glasses for contact lenses, paid for a hair straightening treatment and even started wearing make-up. She had become distant, dry and colourless, but I had already guessed that outside the house, she was a very different

Dounia.

The summer she turned 20, my big sister announced that she would no longer be joining us for the traditional family holiday back in the old country.

Her decision to forgo our annual return to the bled marked a breaking point for my parents. Up until then, they had both been hoping this was a passing phase.

'It's called an "adolescent crisis".'

'What's that? A virus? A disease?'

'It's the kind of disease you can only catch in Europe! If you hadn't brought me here, and we had raised them in Algeria instead, Dounia would never have caught it!'

'Yes, but if I hadn't brought you here, then, at this time of day, you'd be milking a cow, feeding the hens, washing the laundry in the oued and fetching drinking water from the well!'

'That's enough of your silly ideas! You know perfectly well they don't live like that anymore. They're doing better than we are. Algerians are the Americans of the Mahgreb. Do you want to hear my view? If you hadn't brought me here, I would see my family every day, and I'd be able to gaze at the lemon trees and almond trees I planted in my garden instead of watching *Stop* signs springing up alongside rusty washing machines.'

At the time, I was just a kid who liked re-enacting the Trojan war in the garden, but I remember that when my sister distanced herself from us, something snapped in our family.

I loved Dounia because she asked my opinion on lots of matters, and her wallet was stuffed full of cash. There were so many notes sticking out of it I thought she was a millionaire. She bought me my first console and paid for the occasional trip to the cinema.

While forging a brilliant university career, Dounia was a waitress at *La Cour des Miracles*, a smart brassiere in the centre of town.

One Saturday, she took me there after I had promised not to breathe a word to our parents. She didn't want them finding out, because back then she still felt guilty. My father didn't lack for set ideas about things. In his eyes, a waitress was a prostitute with a tray in her hand and an apron round her waist. It goes without saying that I kept the secret out of loyalty, but also because I was dreaming of her buying me that pair of Adidas Stan Smiths for when I started secondary school.

Dounia had a new group of girlfriends who were customers at the brasserie. They drank white wine and left lipstick smears on the rims of their stemmed glasses. I remember the way they laughed as they exhaled their cigarette smoke, which seemed to fill every nook and cranny. They wore short skirts and one of them kept asking another: 'Do you think he'll, like, call me back? But like, do you actually think he will, though? Call me?'

A group of 20-year-old Julie Guérins had helped awaken my sister's inner 'Christine'.

I bet these girls wouldn't go down well with Maman, I thought to myself as I watched them.

And then, on my way back from the toilets, I noticed Dounia hastily putting down a glass of wine and passing a lit cigarette to one of the Julies at the table. 'Don't pull that face!' she said to me, looking embarrassed and miming 'Shhh!' with a finger to her lips, followed by a conspiratorial wink. Aged ten, I was shocked.

I was silent on the bus, on the way home from *La Cour des Miracles*.

'Why aren't you talking, Mourad?'

'No reason.'

'Is it because you saw me drinking?'

I feigned interest in what was going on at the back of the bus. I felt betrayed.

'Yes. And smoking too!'

'It's your own fault, you shouldn't pee so fast... Anyway, don't mention it to anyone, okay? Promise?'

'All right, promise, I won't say anything.'

'...'

'Dounia?'

'What?'

'Do you eat pork as well?'

'Pork? You're sick in the head!'

'Dounia?'

'What now?'

'Are you going to buy me my pair of Stan Smiths?'

'Fine, all right, I get it. So, here's the deal, don't breathe a word to anyone and we'll go to the sports shop next week, okay?'

She gave me that conspiratorial wink again, which was starting to bug me.

Three pairs of years went by. Dounia qualified with flying colours and fulfilled her ambition of becoming a lawyer. Despite the tense atmosphere at home, my mother wanted to bring us together over a special meal.

Food, always. Her way of celebrating her daughter's success. Deep down she was proud, even if, as soon as Dounia announced that she had been called to the bar in Nice a few days earlier, Maman remarked, 'I don't see what all the fuss is about when, at your age, you're still not married...!'

The chicken tagine with olives had gone cold. Dounia was

too offended to show up. My mother's blood pressure had risen to 170 over 60 and she risked having one of her turns. Big Baba wandered into the garden and started nervously pulling out the long grass by the path.

It was all too much for my mother. Apart from a few tactless remarks, she didn't understand what she had done to deserve this.

'I've tried my best to make my children happy! Her problem is that she wishes she'd been born into a different family! She's always been jealous of other people! Deep down, she'd like to be a Frenchie! That's the truth of the matter!'

Mina, who had been close to Dounia in childhood, barely spoke to her these days. She was growing bitter about the sister she considered as the root of all our troubles.

Especially on one day in September 2001: Tuesday 11th September 2001, to be precise. I was 16 with a layer of fluff on my upper lip. Although I'd wanted to shave that morning, but I'd decided to wait a bit longer before becoming a man.

The whole planet was in a state of shock, and so were we. Far from New York, another dramatic scene was unfolding, a far-reaching and catastrophic attack on our family life.

Dounia had packed her bags. There was a car in front of the house, with its engine running and the boot open. I peeked through the living room curtains.

A hotshot young lawyer sat in the driver's seat. Hanging off a wrist, as hairy as it was skinny, shone an enormous watch that could have told the time all the way to the other end of the street. On his nose, a pair of sunglasses designed for skiing. He looked ridiculous, not to mention disconcerting because he kept glancing in my direction, and I had no way of telling whether he could see that I could see him. When he waved at me, I closed the curtain hastily.

'At least he understands me,' Dounia's shrill voice rang out in the hallway. 'None of you understand me, and you never will.'

My mother's hand gestures conveyed her sense of powerlessness.

Mina's lips were quivering with emotion.

'You're the one who doesn't understand anything. Aren't you ashamed of putting our parents through this? You have to make everybody suffer with your lousy selfishness. Go on, do it then, clear off with your boyfriend, you lousy sell-out. And leave us in peace. We're better off without you.'

'My daughter! Why are you doing this? Why?'

My mother clutched her chest so tightly I thought her hand would dig a passage to her heart.

'It's not like anybody's going to miss me if I leave. You've never loved me, anyway.'

'It's the devil whispering evil things to you! Don't leave, my daughter!'

'Let her walk out on us, Maman. Good riddance.'

'If I'd let you have your way, you'd have slammed the brakes on my life. That's the truth of the matter. Well, from now on I'm going to own my life and be free! I won't let you choose a husband for me or lock me up inside this house.'

Crash!

Mina, who was close at hand, managed to cushion my mother's fall.

'Quick, Mourad! A glass of water! A glass of water!'

Don't forget to picture all this happening in Mexican soap opera mode.

My father, who hadn't reacted up until that point, finally spoke, 'If you leave this house, you're never coming back.'

'I've already chosen between you and Daniel, and he wins hands down!'

Crash!

Big Baba landed on a chair in the living room.

There were tears in Dounia's eyes as she walked away, but she never looked back; her emaciated body dragging a suitcase that appeared to weigh a tonne. I made to help her, but my father restrained me, putting his hand on my shoulder. I watched my sister disappear into the car together with that extra-heavy suitcase, Daniel, his hairy wrists and his enormous watch.

So that was how Dounia left us, having waited in vain for my parents to love her *the right way*. Nobody saw her again for nearly ten years.

Mina and Me

Our paternal grandfather lived to 103 on a diet of bread, honey, figs and olives. He had beautiful blue eyes that pierced our mountains to the West, and a beard as white as freshly harvested cotton. Sidi Ahmed Chennoun was the most handsome old man I have ever beheld. He made a point of crouching down when talking to us, and, at his request, he ate his meals at the children's table.

He was full of stories. He'd lived long enough to experience different eras: witnessing wars and the changing of currencies; travelling by donkey as well as by train; communicating via telegram and then the mobile phone. When we were little, what astonished us most was that he also spoke French and even German.

During our holidays in Algeria, Mina and I loved watching him perform his early morning ablutions in the household courtyard, before making his dawn prayer.

Grandfather wasn't afraid of dying. Today, I have a better understanding of why, but at the time I failed to grasp his faith and humility. He died a few years later, prostrated in prayer.

It was the first time I'd lost someone close to me. There had been that TV presenter who hosted a midday game show on France 1. I'd felt sad when he'd gone, but it was different.

With my grandfather, I pictured him closing his blue eyes

for the last time, and I wondered, *So does everything just stop?*

Sidi Ahmed Chennoun was much loved. From what we were told, hundreds of people attended his burial.

Big Baba was furious he couldn't be there. It happened during the first two weeks of July and all the flights on Air Algeria were full. An airline employee tapped away at her computer keyboard, her up-do stiff with hairspray.

'I'm sorry, Monsieur Chennoun, but there's no availability,' she said, noisily chewing gum. 'Not a single seat. All the flights are booked out. It's a shame, because if your father had passed on even two days earlier, you could've had a seat on the 12.55.... You're fresh out of luck!'

Big Baba didn't find this easy to swallow.

Staring at the jobsworth in front of him, who was displaying zero sensitivity in response to his difficult bereavement, he asked, 'Who raised you to behave like that? Donkeys? Dogs?'

Mina has always been very influenced by our grandfather. Out of all of us, she's the one who evokes his memory most often.

She has a soft spot for old people. As a teenager, she used to spend her Wednesdays playing Scrabble at the local care home in Colline-Fleurie, behind the town hall. Back at ours afterwards, the smell of hairspray and second-hand clothes would cling to her.

She's worked there ever since, and that same smell still lingers about her person. She plays the same games of Scrabble, even if her former opponents are all deceased.

At 20, Mina met Jalil, a healthcare assistant who worked at the same care home and who didn't hang about when it came to asking for her hand in marriage.

On their engagement day, he brought his brothers, his parents, his sister, his mother's neighbour who had doubled as his wet nurse, his cousin by marriage and more guests than I can remember. We could have ushered the Rolling Stones into our living room, and no one would have paid them any attention. There were so many cars parked up in front of our gate, it looked like a Bastille Day military parade; with almost as many people, and just as much protocol.

My future brother-in-law, Jalil, and his family brought trays piled high with honey pastries, as well as presents for Mina, fabric for my mother, and plenty of money and noise. When they sang, some of them waved their handkerchiefs, others mini Algerian flags. When the older women ululated, they stuck their tongues right out to make their shameless high-pitched youyous. I remember my father staring at me and cracking a joke: 'Watch out, cowboys! Here come the Indians!' It was meant to ease the tension. He threw back his head and laughed, his fillings gleaming at the back of his mouth. He hadn't laughed much since Dounia's big departure.

As well as the usual biros clipped into his shirt pocket, Big Baba had insisted on my mother tying his best stripy tie, and he'd also decided to wear his pair of ex-shop-display spectacles, the ones with plastic lenses that were a gift from our pharmacist neighbour.

Now, I'd just like to point out that he didn't have any problems with his eyesight. No, he wore those glasses perched on the end of his nose to give him a superior edge and to complete his important-and-respectable outfit. They were his accessory of choice whenever he had to deal with the authorities, attend a school meeting, or visit a travel agency;

and then there were special occasions such as this.

As I stared at him in his tweed jacket that was too tight across the shoulders, it occurred to me that this was the person he would like to have been. Someone with a PhD in quantum physics, aloof and long-sighted, who felt comfortable everywhere and could hold his own with people from all walks of life.

Big Baba had done his best to impress Mina's in-laws, but the natural joker in him hadn't wasted any time in resurfacing. He monopolised the conversation all afternoon, with a catalogue of embarrassing stories that made my mother blush. No sooner had they left than she gave him a piece of her mind: a process which, as usual, took hours.

'Always leaving me with h'chouma on my face. You're like a language-mill, flinging out words.'

'You were ashamed? You must be joking! They were begging for more, I'm telling you!'

'They were too polite to say anything, but they'd had enough of your jokes, and as for those stories of yours that send everyone to sleep standing up!'

'Nonsense, they loved them! It was lucky I was there to entertain them; if I'd left it to you, everyone would have died of boredom!'

'You wouldn't let me get a word in edgeways! You didn't draw breath all day! The moment you finished one story you started on another. You were talking so much it made them thirsty!'

'Pfff... It's taken me nearly 30 years of marriage to notice how jealous you are! Too bad!'

'Did you really need to tell them about tinkering with the taxi meters back in Algeria? Or the mule you sold for 15,000 dinars to those poor Germans?'

'They laughed so hard when I told them the one about

the Germans! And it's thanks to those scams I paid for our wedding!'

'And you're proud? It's our marriage that's the scam! And I'm the donkey for agreeing to marry you! Tfffou! Who knows if they'll ever come back again, after those stupid stories! Mina will end up an old maid, because of you!'

My parents have always been crazy about each other. This kind of verbal sparring would spice up their daily lives, like a dash of harissa lifting a bland dish. It's funny, when you think they were married without ever having clapped eyes on one another.

It would be fair to say that Mina chose a different path to Dounia's. You'd think she had sworn to do the exact opposite. My theory is that she was afraid of letting our parents down, when it came to her turn. Family is sacred for her.

I can still picture the day when the imam conducted her religious marriage. She and Jalil have three children now. A girl and two boys: Khadija, Mohamed and Abou Bakr. My mother says they've got baraka, in other words they're lucky: 'God gave them a talent for it. Mina is fertile!'

When Mina told her she was pregnant for the third time, Maman replied, 'Alhamdulillah! That's good news! But tell me, my daughter, what do you eat? Compost?'

They set up home two streets away from our house. Jalil understands how close Mina needs to be to my mother. And vice versa.

Over time, Mina became the new big sister. She qualified as a healthcare assistant, specialising in geriatric care out of her love for the third age, and when she went back to work, she left the children with their grandmother, who was overjoyed with this arrangement.

A balance had been struck without 'That One'; which is

what we called Dounia, on the rare occasions when we still mentioned her.

As for me, after a year of toiling in the dark, like Chinese child labour in a Nike factory, I finally passed the CAPES. As in, the Certificate of Aptitude for Secondary School Teaching. I'm unpacking that acronym because I want every word to sink in.

I mean, holy shit. That's some feat.

It was the seventh of July. My mother was frying aubergines. The smell of oil was seeping into everything, including the fibres of my T-shirt, which was already drenched in sweat. I was on the Publinet website, where they post the list of newly qualified secondary school teachers. The verdict was due at midday, and still nothing. Every minute, my trembling index finger clicked again to refresh the results page. It felt as if I sat there staring at the screen for an eternity, my eyes dilated like a junkie's after their fix.

Adrenaline rushes are rare for someone like me: a guy nothing ever happens to.

And then, finally, I saw my name appear. I'd never felt so proud of that name. I stood up slowly, silently, and I was crying as I rubbed the back of my head. But I was quick to wipe away my tears. Big Baba says men don't cry, and it's always stuck with me.

It was reassuring to see my surname, followed by 'Pass'. I was going to do something with my life.

At last, I could delete the cringe-making film that haunted me. A nightmare in which I had no social life, no job, and no friends.

In that film, I play an obese saddo with salt-and-pepper hair. I'm drowning in cooking fat and I still live in my parents' house when I'm long past 50. My mum handwashes my underwear and cuts my toenails, because I've become too fat and too lazy to do it myself. I spend my days reading books I've already read, what with the effort of dragging my lardy body outside to borrow new tomes from the library.

I banished those gross images, and I prayed to God to save me from salt-and-pepper hair.

Solitude had led me to a love books, and now I was going to teach French literature.

My mother wanted to organise a big meal to celebrate my success.

Food, always.

She offered to make couscous. I remember wondering at the time whether she'd become superstitious about avoiding chicken tagine with olives.

'You should invite your friends!' my mother suggested, much to my surprise. Trouble was, I didn't have any.

There was Raoul Wong, a former classmate and one of my few school friends to have found favour in Maman's eyes, back in the day.

'It's good to have a Chinese friend! The Chinese work hard and don't borrow other people's pens. They're calm and clean, and you never see them loitering outside. And another thing, they're good with computers! In a few years, they'll have the power, they'll beat the Americans, and everyone will speak Chinese! You mark my words!'

Unluckily for me, Raoul Wong moved away last summer.

'Well, Mourad? Have you decided how many people you'd like to invite?'

'Not yet, Maman, I'll think about it.'

'Roughly how many... 10, 20, 30?'

'I don't know yet, Maman.'

I was playing for time. What if I randomly invited 20

strangers I found online?

It was a source of sorrow for my mother that I was a loner. She had assumed, by turns, that I suffered from anxiety, or a personality disorder, or that I was gay.

But none of the above applied. I was a loner. End of. And I'd come to terms with it. Not that I think she understood the leading role she had played in the story of my social withdrawal. Nobody is solitary by nature.

Apart from Raoul Wong, my mother had never liked any of my friends. She criticised them all to the point of putting me off them too. As for girls, let's not even go there. Nothing, and nobody, was good enough for her son.

One day, when I was in Year 11, Harry came to our home with his Super Nintendo to play *Donkey Kong Country*. Big Baba had given his permission.

Harry was the popular kid at our lycée. His clothes were sharp and he made everybody laugh. I couldn't believe my luck when he agreed to come to my house with his console.

If I should ever stand beneath the golden canopy of the Republic, for the honour of being awarded a medal, I would probably feel less overwhelmed than I did that Wednesday afternoon when I saw Harry on our front doorstep.

'You've got too many fake flowers in your house,' Harry pointed out, as we walked through the living room. I was on such a high I didn't even feel offended.

Then he became very serious and explained how the controls worked, before starting the game. I kept losing, falling into ravines and being bumped off by two-headed enemies.

Every so often, it got on Harry's nerves that he'd picked such a rubbish gamer, but I was having the time of my life.

We'd only been playing for an hour when my mother came storming into my bedroom.

'Right! That's enough of these games! Switch everything off! Harry, it's time for you to go home. Mourad has his homework to do. You may have parents who can read French, who can help you revise for your exams, who can find you an internship, a job, a nice place to live. But Mourad will have to get ahead by the sweat of his own brow. He's going to have to work twice as hard! Come on, unplug everything, *now!*'

Then she stared at Harry's feet.

'And you haven't even taken off your shoes! Didn't anyone teach you to take off your shoes off before going into other people's houses? Tfffou! I suppose you pay for a cleaner at your place?'

'No, Madame Chennoun.'

'Well, in that case, it must be very dirty indeed!'

The poor guy was petrified. He stuffed his console into his backpack and cleared off. I stayed where I was without uttering a word. My knees were trembling.

It goes without saying, Harry never came back to our house. If we passed each other in the school corridors, he'd give me a pitying look, but he never spoke to me again. I bet he had nightmares about my mother. In horror movie mode.

Sequence I – Interior night – Deathly silence. A backdrop of plastic flowers. An overweight woman enters the room; she resembles a hysterical horse about to be given a lethal injection. Her mauve headscarf is poorly adjusted and she is wielding a magnifying glass as her weapon.

My mother had made baghrirs that day, Algerian-style pancakes.

When I was alone at last, I didn't want anyone to hear me

crying, so I pressed my face into the pillow. Yes, Big Baba had drummed it into my head once and for all: Men. Don't. Cry.

Thankfully, my father came home not long after and he could tell that something was up.

Perhaps the pancakes left an aftertaste. In any event, Big Baba had no trouble in making me spit out the story. It was the only time I saw him genuinely lose his temper with my mother. He thought her behaviour was shameful.

'What on earth came over you? And what about the boy's parents? What are they going to think? That we're uneducated savages!'

'Their son already has a savings account that's full to bursting! They couldn't care less.'

'What are you talking about?! And why are you being so headstrong? Can't you see how unhappy you're making the boy? He's 16. He's not a baby anymore. Do you want him to walk out on us as well?! At this rate, he'll have packed his bags by the time he's 18! And don't come complaining to me when he does! Do you want to drive them all away?'

'What are you trying to say? Go on, out with it...'

'You've understood!'

'I've only got one son! One! I want him to focus on his future! I don't want him keeping the wrong sort of company! Is that a crime?'

'The wrong sort of company? The boy brought a video game round to our house! The way you're talking, anyone would think you'd caught them selling drugs!'

'Listen, it starts with video games and, before you know it, we're talking syringes and police custody! Do you begrudge me wishing the best for my child? Eh? Am I a bad mother, in your eyes?'

Big Baba tapped his index finger on his forehead, as if to

say, *You've got a screw loose.* My mother was beside herself. She kept gasping for breath as she returned to her cooking, the tears pouring down her neck.

That's why I didn't put up a fight. I never put up a fight. For fear of increasing her palpitations, her blood pressure, her hyperglycaemia, or triggering some other drama.

I learnt to be alone. Sometimes, I even got a kick out of being bored.

On weekends when the weather was fine, I perched on Big Baba's referee's chair, at the bottom of the garden, and buried my nose in a book instead of heading into town.

I would read for hours on end, especially in summer. With the sun beating down on my forehead, I'd read until I couldn't take the heat any more, at which point I'd climb down and pour myself some homemade citronnade.

As the years went by, I became increasingly isolated. I even came round to the idea that my mother wasn't completely wrong.

After all, guys my age only have one thing on their minds: making the beast-with-two-backs in the rear of their three-door Twingo with P for Provisional Driver plates. In the evenings, there's always a party at someone's apartment, and a shy girl chewing the edge of her plastic cup waiting for someone to hit on her.

Student discounts aside, I didn't have much in common with my peers.

I was at one remove, picturing them in 20 years' time with a mortgage, driving around in a family estate car, plucking up the courage to ask for their next salary rise, even if it meant pandering to their pot-bellied boss and his condescending attitude.

I wasn't under any illusions: it was unlikely that I'd be allocated a local teaching post.

More teachers applied to work in and around Nice than almost anywhere else. Priority was given to experienced teachers, married teachers, teachers with kids, and those who were all of the above.

It's probably the same with the police. Fast forward to the guy with the Marseilles accent and the freshly issued police uniform who finds himself in the banlieues north-east of Paris, patrolling the forlorn tarmac of the gritty 93 postcode. He'll bring a ray of Provençal sunshine to an ID check that's turning nasty.

Big Baba was worried about me leaving the south for the start of the new academic year.

'There's a 12-year-old kid in Seine-Saint-Denis who stabbed his History and Geography teacher for giving him a bad mark!'

My mother couldn't resist wading in.

'If I'd known you were going to be a teacher, we'd have gone back to Algeria after your father retired. At least they respect the teaching profession over there...'

'Respect? On 30,000 dinars a month? That's less than they pay their refuse collectors! Stop talking nonsense, Djamila!'

'I don't mean the salary! I mean the students! In Algeria, no student would ever dare to throw a book or a piece of chalk in the teacher's face, let alone attack them the way they do here!'

'Of course, they wouldn't! They haven't got any books, or any chalk!'

'Stop talking nonsense, yourself! You always exaggerate! Tfffou!'

I felt guilty every time I gave my parents cause to worry. In our family, Mina was the only one who didn't make waves.

'What was I like when I was a little girl, Maman?'

'Why do you want to know?'

'I'm just curious. The kids ask me sometimes.'

'I don't remember, benti, you were kind. The same as you are now. You were a good girl.'

'Didn't I ever do anything silly?'

'Not that I can remember. You were always sensible.'

'What about at school, wasn't I ever in trouble?'

'No. Now I come to think about it, I don't remember you being in trouble. You were a nice kid at school. "Nothing to report!" your teachers used to say. Mourad, on the other hand, was always getting into trouble, that's for sure! One day, he climbed up onto the primary school roof and stayed there for hours, like a cat! The headmistress telephoned me. I remember having palpitations, I thought my chest would burst! "Madame Chennoun," she said, "Could you tell me why Mourad isn't in class today?" And I said: "What do you mean, not in class? Of course he's in class, I dropped him off at eight o'clock this morning!" My God, I'll never forget that day! It turned into a kidnap alert! I kept thinking about those men who open their raincoats in front of schoolchildren to expose their private parts. I said to myself, *Our Mourad's so wet behind the ears, he must have taken sweets from a stranger and climbed into a white van!* The police combed the neighbourhood. And then we found him, about ten o'clock that night, fast asleep on the school roof. I screamed. The shame of it! People must have thought: "They don't have a bed at home!"'

'Yes, I remember, Maman, the story made it onto the regional TV news, and you recorded it so you could send the cassette to Algeria ...'

'What do you expect? It was the first time anyone in our family had been on telly.'

The Article

I wasn't the only person in our family to interest the press.

That morning, Big Baba looked irritable on his return from the covered market, and I don't mean in a can-you-believe-the-price-of-tomatoes kind of way. Feverishly, he unbuttoned his khaki coat and took off his black fur hat. In winter, I've always maintained he looks like a Russian army colonel with that karakul on his head.

He was frowning as he held out the newspaper, which he had carefully folded in four and tucked inside his jacket pocket.

'Take a look at that.'

It was a copy of *Nice Matin*. On the front page, in the bottom-left inset, was a photo of my sister Dounia. The first thing I noticed was her strikingly short haircut. It suited her.

'Well? Why is her photo in the newspaper? Is she dead?'

My father's frozen expression made me realise he wasn't so much irritated as beside himself with worry.

'No, Papa. She isn't dead.'

His eyes said *phew*, but his mouth said, 'Anyway, it's as if she *is* dead to me...'

After a long silence, he added, 'What does it say about her? Read it to me.'

There was just a short paragraph. And the photo.

'Read it in a journalist's voice.'

Big Baba always asked me to help him out whenever he needed to read something: Doctor Zerbib's prescriptions, a leaflet from the CGT general workers union, articles from *Healthy Ageing*, letters from the bank, or else the catalogues with supermarket special offers.

And for each document, no matter how different, he was adamant that I read it 'in a journalist's voice'.

Headline. *Daring to be Diverse: The New Team of Councillors.*

Underneath. *Spotlight on Dounia Chennoun, Mayor Yves Peplinski's trump card in his bid to attract new voters as he stands for re-election. This 36-year-old lawyer, born to Algerian immigrant parents, is as ambitious as she is determined. Following her involvement with the controversial feminist organisation* 'Speak Out Sister!', *she's one to watch at the start of a promising political career.*

Don't forget to register on the electoral list before Saturday 31st December, blah blah blah...

'What do you mean blah blah blah? Is that all?

'Yes, that's all, Papa.'

'Why did they write "born to immigrant parents"? Why didn't they just put "lawyer"?'

We heard my mother turning the keys in the lock. She was back from the school fair with Mina and the kids. Mohamed and Abou Bakr both had their faces painted as tigers and Khadija was sporting a ladybird look.

'How does this stuff wash off? My sink's going to be unspeakable by the time you've all rinsed your faces!

'Don't worry! I'll deal with it, Maman!'

'Thank you, benti!'

The little ones gave Big Baba a kiss.

With vibrant colours on his cheeks, half tiger, half ladybird, he turned towards me and his eyes flashed, *Let's keep this information secret!*

Yes, Big Baba has eyes that speak.

I folded the newspaper discretely and slipped it into my jeans pocket. My mother sailed into the living room, one eyebrow raised in a quizzical circumflex while the other sloped in a frown. It's what she does if she suspects something. She's a woman with a talent for pulling faces.

'What are you both up to? You look like you're plotting a military coup in Africa!'

Neither of us responded. She untied her scarf, still looking suspicious. Then she pointed at Big Baba.

'What are you scheming, Abdelkader? Are you planning on taking a second wife? Eh? Is that it?'

Big Baba gave a big belly laugh, worthy of a studio audience member falling off their seat during the recording of an extra-tacky Benny Hill sketch.

'A second wife? Are you kidding me? You're as much trouble as four wives. I've reached the max just with you!'

At least we knew where to find Dounia now. But from there to voting for her... let's not get carried away.

This city has been right-wing since the Stone Age. It wouldn't surprise me if Peplinski croaked in office. He's like an Africa-style president for the Provence-Alpes-Côte d'Azur region.

No amount of piecing together scraps of memories could help me to understand my sister's turnaround. To be actively engaged in right-wing politics, in a council with more varicose veins and incontinence than ideas and electoral promises? That's not the Dounia I know.

I've lost track of the number of times I'd tried to imagine Dounia's life, following her dramatic departure.

Was she still in France? Did she have children? And if

so, how many? Did she end up marrying Daniel, with his hairy wrists and enormous watch? Or had she decided on something radically different? I'd made a list of wild guesses about what might have happened to her.

Perhaps she'd moved to Brazil to fight against deforestation. Or to somewhere in Peru to defend bankrupted farmers. Perhaps she had become an ambassador for UNESCO and travelled around India promoting education for young girls? But no. Not a bit of it. Turns out she had moved a few kilometres up the road, and now, in the name of the 'diversity' she supposedly represents, she's at number eight on the list as part of the team to get that old alcoholic Yves Peplinski re-elected as mayor, for his 250th mandate.

End of. Talk about an anti-climax.

The Diagnosis

One look at Doctor Zerbib would tell you where Big Baba sourced his inspiration for dressing up as a respectable intellectual. Their outfits were almost identical. Tweed jacket, corduroy trousers, striped tie and glasses so far down the nose they're on the brink of committing suicide. Not forgetting the Bic biros, of course, clipped to the shirt pocket.

The biggest difference between Big Baba and Zerbib, apart from years of studies, was probably personal hygiene. I don't think our family doctor washed his hair very often. I remember he was forever dusting off his shoulders, so you felt like you were inside a paperweight snow globe, without the fairy tale.

Big Baba liked things that were old and reassuring: my mother, the junk piled up in our garden, his Renault R11 turbo and his black fur karakul. Which explains why nothing in the world could have persuaded him to choose a different GP.

Doctor Zerbib's surgery was always open, except for Shabbat. He refused to use a computer, he had one of those colonial-style wooden consulting rooms and he had even organised a regional conference about the damaging effects of automated measuring devices for arterial tension.

'Tfffou! He's a charlatan, that doctor! People only see

Zerbib to get signed off work! Everyone knows that!'

One point to my mother. But that was before the changes to the health benefits system. Patient reimbursements worked differently from then on, Zerbib had the medical insurers breathing down his neck and the era of being signed off work for a fortnight was over. As a result, so many people deserted the practice that, in a matter of months, the average age of his patients went from 45 to 75.

Given the risk of being struck off, Doctor Zerbib became conscientious to a fault. The day he diagnosed my mother as being a hypochondriac, she took against him for good.

'You're perfectly healthy, Madame Chennoun! I bet you'll live to be France's next-oldest citizen! If God wills it so, you'll overtake Jeanne Calment and her 122 years!'

'So, what are you prescribing me? Peppermints?'

'No, Madame Chennoun, homeopathy. You're just a little bit anxious. These will calm you down and help you to sleep better.'

'That's it? And you're asking me for €22, Dr Zerbib?'

'23. It's gone up.'

'€23 to tell me I'm hysterical?'

'I didn't say hysterical, I said hypochondriac, let's be clear.'

My mother eventually unearthed a different doctor who didn't balk at issuing her with a wad of prescriptions, and who diagnosed her with diabetes, hypertension and osteoarthritis.

Thanks to him, she won the ultimate argument for the rest of her days: the state undertook to pay 100 percent of all medical expenses in recognition of her long-term incapacity.

On the bus: 'Excuse me, young man, could I have your seat please? I'm on 100 percent!'

At the supermarket till: 'Sorry, but do you mind if I go ahead of you? I'm on 100 percent!'

To my father: 'Stop getting on my nerves, Abdelkader! I'm on 100 percent!'

Despite all the doubts concerning Marc Zerbib's competence as a doctor, Big Baba remained his most loyal patient.

Until the day he said to Mina, 'I've got a very bad headache.'

It was rare for Big Baba to complain. Mina gave him some paracetamol and a glass of water and told the children to play quietly. That was when she noticed my father was struggling to raise the glass to his mouth.

'What's going on, Papa?'

Big Baba was staring into space.

We rang Doctor Zerbib, who recommended the patient rest up for a few days while we waited on a scan appointment.

But the reality was that Big Baba was suffering a stroke, otherwise known as a cerebrovascular accident. CVA: three letters that conceal a life-threatening emergency.

When my mother noticed that Big Baba's right arm was swelling up, she remembered hearing from a neighbour about her sister's father-in-law, who had suffered a stroke back in Algeria...

Long story short, we called the emergency services and rushed straight to hospital.

Half of Big Baba

It was July and, just like every summer, old ladies with facelifts were well represented in Nice. They're a protected species in the Alpes-Maritimes.

And easy enough to spot.

Most of the time they spit-roast their knees on the benches along Promenade des Anglais, flaunting outsize Dior glasses and hideous platinum blond hair that's been backcombed and scraped into a chignon. You often see them trailing a scrawny mutt on a leather leash and wearing garish colours that clash with their age.

They helped me to realise, no matter how wealthy you are, money can't buy you taste.

The ambulance was speeding across town. My mother gripped Big Baba's hand and kept asking him if he could feel anything. The atmosphere was out of sync with the frivolous mood outside in the street, where tourists were strolling in breathable sandals.

Big Baba lay on his stretcher, staring out of the window. He could glimpse a patch of blue sky and a few palm branches dancing to the rhythm of the siren and the revolving light. From that angle, he could have been taking in the sea front in Algiers.

Surprise, surprise, Peplinski had been re-elected, and the faded posters still clung to nearly every traffic light post. My sister had been put in charge of Youth Services at Nice City Council. In any other city, this would have been a great opportunity, but in Nice... youth? What youth?

Nice is the only city in the world where I've heard people talk about 'a young person of 50-something'.

We were approaching Nice University Hospital, closely followed by Jalil in the grey Renault Scenic. When Big Baba was admitted to the Neurovascular Unit, my mother went into shock. She kept readjusting her headscarf as we followed the two male nurses who had taken over from the paramedics. They carefully transferred Big Baba onto a trolley. One of them was wearing an earring in the shape of Guadeloupe.

We rushed down a long corridor punctuated by several swing doors with porthole windows. It all felt strangely familiar. I'd watched this scene hundreds of times before, in umpteen hospital dramas on countless TV repeats.

The shaved head of the other nurse was covered in beads of sweat and he kept saying: 'Mind out!' to anyone in the way of our convoy.

A young doctor ran up to join us from behind. He wore a ponytail and fluorescent sandals and his eyebrows met in the middle, which gave him a disturbing look. He wanted to understand what had happened and began to barrage us with stress-inducing questions. We could have been participating in a TV family quiz show; all that was missing was the red buzzer and the weekend-for-two somewhere you've never even heard of.

His badge informed me that he was called Doctor Freddy Gerard.

Things were not looking good. In just a few hours Big

Baba's entire right side, including his face, had become paralysed. His mouth sagged and his eyelid drooped until it was almost shut. It was a scary sight.

The blurred vision and speech loss observed on admission, however, hadn't persisted. On that front, Freddy was reassuring.

After hours of waiting, and very few updates on Big Baba's condition, we were all jittery.

In the reception area, I emptied the grubby coffee machine of its tar juice, while Jalil kept the children busy with a game of dominos he'd found in the glove compartment of his car. My mother was crying and her khol eyeliner was running. Mina was crying and her khol eyeliner was running too. 'Is Pépé dead?' Khadija asked.

On the metal seats opposite us in the waiting room, a skinny teenage girl sat tightly wedged between her parents; the three of them reminded me of the expression 'joined at the hip'.

We saw a bunch of white coats go past, followed by figures in blue, pink and green. Some were heading outside to smoke, while others were just passing through.

A patient with facial burns wandered around the reception area looking distraught. He came up to me and said, 'I'd have become an artist, if it weren't for these ten bone idle fingers!' I made a mental note to remember that line.

At last, Doctor Freddy came back to see us, with his toolkit of complicated medical terms. Words so technical they appeared to float in front of my mother's face.

'I'm sorry, but we didn't bring a dictionary with us, and none of us has a PhD...' said Mina, running out of patience. 'So, could you talk normally, please? Using simple words!'

We were allowed to go and see Big Baba. Two at a time. Room 314.

My mother and I opened the door and were assailed by a noxious odour: the stench of urine mingling with the whiff of sanitizing gel. This played out against a soundtrack of electrocardiograms and nurses' clogs on clean lino.

Seeing Big Baba frail and flat on his back, I couldn't help picturing him dead. Just thinking about it gave me a sharp pain in my chest.

I immediately banished the idea.

Instead, I found myself asking the stupid question you ask anyway:

'Are you okay?'

He blinked slowly. Only one of his eyes closed shut. I took this to mean yes.

Youth and Health

Big Baba was only half alive. Hemiplegic, to use the medical term.

A month had gone by since his stroke and he had just been transferred to the hospital's 'Neuro Rehab' unit. There were no obvious signs of progress, but he was still here. Half was good enough for us.

Nice was in the grip of a heatwave. On some days, the temperature soared to 41 degrees. I was on three showers a day, minimum.

'Hey! Mourad! The water in the bathroom isn't for free, you know! It doesn't just fall out of the sky!'

'Oh yes it does, Maman.'

'I suppose you think you're funny? Tfffou!'

The days ticked by, but the heart had gone out of our home.

We no longer ate our evening meal at eight o'clock on the dot. There was no fruit in the glass dish on the living room table, and the neighbourhood cats had stopped roaming in our garden now their doting benefactor was no longer around to feed them.

I was finally allocated my first teaching job. The wait was over. As I had suspected, I would be working as a newly qualified teacher in the Paris region. In Montreuil, to be specific, east of the city, in the department of Seine-Saint-Denis, at the Collège Gustave-Courbet. When I read the name of the school in my posting letter, it immediately conjured embarrassing images of that close-up on female intimacy in Gustave Courbet's famous painting: *The Origins of the World*.

But I had a more serious problem on my hands: finding somewhere to stay. With less than a month to go.

It was Maman's idea to telephone cousin Miloud.

After arriving in Paris two or three years earlier, with a student visa and a place at Paris-XIII University, Miloud had decided to stay on despite his provisional residence permit expiring.

Mina was against it. As were the authorities.

'Are you serious? You're talking about Miloud? Miloud the glue-sniffer?'

'Why do you have to bring that up, Mina? He didn't know what he was doing back then, he was a child, meskine!'

'What d'you mean, *poor thing*? You're defending him now! So, you're saying he was a child when he went to prison for pimping a 16-year-old girl in the suburbs of Algiers, on the pavements of Chéraga, right?'

'We don't know the whole story! And anyway, he's changed! He's taken up studying again, and he came to France for a new life... You don't spare anybody, do you?'

'You can't mean that, Maman? Pfff. The guy's a piece of scum. He's a hobo! He disgusts me.'

'We're not asking him to raise your brother! We just want him to put a roof over Mourad's head for two or three weeks until he finds his own studio.'

'Have you signed up online, Mourad?'

'I've taken a fine tooth-comb to the Internet, but from what I can see everything's too expensive.'

'Don't worry, we'll help you out. What about sharing?'
'I'm still looking.'
'That's why we said... *in the meantime, there's always Miloud.*'
'No, Maman! Not Miloud!'

My posting was taking up all our headspace. As a result, we were less preoccupied with Big Baba. We took it in turns with the hospital visits. Although he was glad to see me, I always left on a low. He had no idea how serious his condition was, and I was endlessly rewinding the same cassette.

'I don't know what's going on with this leg. I can't move it!'

'That's what happens when your right side is paralysed, Papa. Don't worry, the physio will sort it out.'

'And my arm as well! Look! I can't even lift it. It feels like someone's pinning me down!'

'Don't worry, Papa.'

'How long is all this going to last?'

'We don't know. The team here is doing everything it can to help you.'

'Perhaps I slept in the wrong position.'

'No, Papa, that's got nothing to do with it. It's because of your stroke. It paralysed your limbs.'

'But why can't I lift my leg?'

'It'll be okay. Don't worry. What matters is there are signs of progress; the doctor told me you've got some feeling in your fingers now...'

'What's my room number?'

'419.'

'Which floor?'

'Fourth. As in 4:19.'

'Look! My leg won't move...'

Then his eyes would cloud with sadness.

'My son, I don't want the nurses to clean me.'

I could picture my grandfather, Sidi Ahmed Chennoun, saying: 'There are only two things we appreciate when we no longer have them: youth and health!'

I'd seen a library signposted on the same floor, and it occurred to me that Big Baba might enjoy it if I read to him.

The library smelled as fusty as a second-hand bookseller (elderly bachelor variety) and consisted of two rickety shelves overrun with yellowed books. There were also a few car magazines with photos of models you would only see in a toyshop window display these days, as collectible miniatures. The educational books and novels must have dated from back when the hospital was still treating patients for the plague.

Oliver Twist was at one dusty end. Oddly enough, when I stared at Dickens from a certain angle, I could detect a faint likeness to Big Baba. The moustache, the serious expression, the slightly anxious gaze, yes, there was something ...

On the shelf below, I spotted the inevitable Harlequin romances... The adrenaline of torrid nights in retirement homes. Authors with white American brush-and-blow-dry names, like Perry Williams or Andrew Richardson. I imagined them as writing stars in Arkansas, collectors of old-fashioned typewriters, divorcees with a weakness for brandy. I could see them, driving their pick-up along a deserted road as they hatched the plot for their next raunchy novel.

I remember writing a school assignment about the role of women in so-called 'romance' literature. I chose *The Captive Mistress*. The title spoke volumes. As did the suggestive cover.

No question of reading anything like that to Big Baba.

So, I opted for the Dickens.

The healthcare assistant came to change my father. As I waited in the corridor, I thought about his sense of modesty;

I thought about how much a man can suffer on becoming a baby again.

'Chapter One. *Treats of the place where Oliver Twist was born, and of the circumstances attending his birth.'*

'Don't forget to read it in a journalist's voice...'

Making Contact

My timetable was as regular as sheet music. In the mornings I lurked online, on the prowl for any friendly-sounding apartment shares, to avoid rooming with my cousin Miloud in some migrant workers' hostel. Or, worse, being accused of aiding and abetting in one of his sex scandals. There was always the option of a damp garret, with a shared toilet on the landing: 800 euros a month, bills not included.

For me, moving to Paris wasn't a dream come true. It simply meant leaving Nice.

In the afternoons, I visited Big Baba. On the menu: a game of Crazy Eights and one rancid cappuccino between the two of us. I always let him win. After all, he could only hold the cards in one hand.

Sometimes, he would turn his head and give a long sigh, before checking everything was running smoothly at home without him.

'Has anyone fixed the leak in the bathroom?'

'You fixed it yourself, Papa... last year.'

'I did?'

'Mourad?' he finally asked, one day.

'Yes, Papa?'

'I want to see my daughter again, before I die.'

'What makes you say that? You're not going to die!'

'Of course, I'm going to die. And I haven't even made my Hajj!'

'Insha'Allah, you'll make a good recovery, Papa. And we'll go to Mecca together. We'll both make our Hajj!'

'I'm starting to forget things. That frightens me. I must see my daughter. I have to see my daughter before I die.'

I can't say it hadn't occurred to me. I'd thought about it every day since Big Baba's stroke. Dounia should know what was going on. Even if Mina and my mother made an impressive show of *business as usual*, I was sure they'd had the same idea too. You can't simply Tippex someone out of the family album.

Big Baba had swallowed his pride. It was time to grab the opportunity before he changed his mind. I resolved not to talk about it to Maman or Mina for the time being.

On the way back from the hospital, I decided to stop off at the town hall. I guess I was acting in the spirit of that expression 'to take potluck'.

I braced myself and parked Big Baba's R11 Turbo in the visitors' car park, before making for the reception where three switchboard operators were in mid-action. Arms flailing, and with the twisted wires of their handsets all tangled up, they looked like they were fronting the office for disorganised octopuses.

The operators smelled like those citrus-scented hand wipes they give you in aeroplanes.

'Hello! Are you here for the job interview?'

'No. I was wondering if... Actually, I've come to see Madame Chennoun.'

'Who should I say is here?'

Mourad Chennoun, I wanted to reply, *son of Abdelkader*

Chennoun, shoemaker of repute, himself the son of Sidi Ahmed Chennoun, poet and shepherd of our mountains to the West.

'Her brother, Mourad.'

That upbeat expression suddenly drained from the operator's face.

'Do you have an appointment?'

'No.'

'Aha! Because she only sees visitors by appointment.'

She had said 'Aha!' conclusively. Meaning, *You stand no chance of seeing her.* I felt like an idiot who had tried ringing Madonna's doorbell on the off-chance.

'It's important.'

'Aha! Did she know you'd be dropping by?'

'No, could you let her know I'm here, please.'

'One moment.'

I detected scorn in the operator's eyes. She had one eyebrow raised in a circumflex while the other sloped in a frown. Just like my mother. Talk about identical scowls. She was wearing blue mascara to match her uniform and, when she dialled, her nails, which were too long to be real, went clickety-clack on the keyboard.

'Hello, Dounia? Your brother's here...'

A long silence and then the operator said 'Aha!' again, before replacing the handset.

'I'm sorry, she can't see you.'

I stood there staring at her and waiting for her to offer me an alternative solution.

'Okay. So what do I do now?'

'Right, well... leave your number, and she'll call you back later.'

What a numbskull! I should have realised it wouldn't be so easy. I mean, it's not like I haven't read enough novels in my time.

Dounia was probably still deeply bitter about everything. How could I have forgotten her level of stubbornness?

I scribbled a note on a small yellow Post-It that had been handed to me by the snippy operator. My message was as spontaneous as it was stupid.

Call me please. Mourad.

After ten years of separation, getting back in touch with a Post-It note was kind of farcical.

'She's got your number, has she?'

The ironic tone led me to suspect that even random switchboard operators wearing citrus-scented perfume knew about our family history. '*Aha*, she must have been thinking, *so here's the evil brother from the evil Arab family that threw Dounia out!*'

I added my mobile number for my sister's benefit.

I didn't write anything about Big Baba's health, or about us. That would have been challenging, on a piece of self-adhesive paper measuring 76 millimetres by 76.

I felt disheartened, but I wasn't ready to leave. For no particular reason, other than to digest my failed attempt at making contact, I stopped in front of the main display area. There was a poster with a Freefone number for victims to speak out against domestic violence. The slogan was striking, to say the least: 'Kill silence, before it kills you.'

It was a campaign by SOS! – the 'Speak Out Sister!' collective headed up by Dounia. SOS! specialised in headline-grabbing slogans, and events that secured maximum media coverage. Ever since we'd picked up the trail of my sister again, I followed SOS! more closely.

Recently, they had even demonstrated in front of the National Assembly to drive home their message and raise awareness amongst politicians. Some of the women had turned up gagged and handcuffed. Others sported bruised faces and black eyes, with bandages wrapped around their heads. A few wore burkas.

On the poster, my sister and the other leaders proudly displayed their banners in red letters with, 'We Won't Be Silenced, For Women's Sake!'

They looked like they were yelling their slogans fit to bust. But deep down, they were probably thinking: 'Here I am, on the frontline, wearing my bright red Dior lipstick. With these killer lips, who says I won't make the front page of *Le Nouvel Obs* on Monday? Yaaaas!'

The anonymous demonstrators at the back were clinging with pained dignity to their placards, and the noble struggle.

One of the collective's most fervent detractors, a man they regularly took to court for defamation, had a blog called: *Shut The Fuck Up, For Everyone's Sake!*

They were always rallying in the name of sisterhood and the bigger cause, but their campaigns felt as phoney to me as Daniel with-the-hairy-wrists wearing ski glasses on a summer's day. The way I saw it, SOS! took advantage of other women's suffering, promoting an image of 'victimhood' to suit their headline-grabbing purposes.

My sister was becoming a symbol. She contributed with increasing regularity to public debates. Whenever she expressed her view on any topic, she did so with breath-taking confidence and poise. The little Arab councillor from the provinces was fast becoming the darling of the Paris elite.

Ahead of earning votes for her future political mandate, she was notching up Air France air miles on all those gas-guzzling Paris-Nice return flights.

Dounia's appeal lies in symbolizing what the Republic does best: producing accidental success stories.

People can't get enough of this model of excellence: 'There you go, if you work hard enough, anything's possible!' It gives them licence to say, 'Easy as one-two-three.' Which makes it seem like everyone else is a waste of space, a bunch of layabouts lacking any ambition to succeed in life.

A fulfilling career?

No thanks. I'd prefer to spend my days buying scratch cards and hanging out at the local betting shop.

A job in a rapidly expanding business?

Not my kind of thing. I'll just complain about my six years of higher education, so people will think I didn't get hired because I was 'overqualified'.

All those lowlifes sponging off the benefits system, lounging about with no sense of shame. It's an outrage!

Politicians, hey? Still, what larks they enjoy in the corridors of power!

Dounia's public image serves these kinds of arguments. I don't know if she's conscious of this. I'd like to have put the question to her, but the switchboard operator just went 'Aha!

I'd watched several YouTube clips featuring my sister. There were some fairly offensive comments posted about Dounia. One that I'd spotted called her a 'corrupt, sell-out, token Arab'.

On my way out, I still kept hoping my sister would change her mind. I sensed someone's eyes drilling into my back and when I turned around I saw the citrus-scented operator shooting me an acidic look. I was convinced that she'd been instructed to inform Dounia as soon as I left the premises. I surrendered.

Out on the boulevard, the police were stopping cars. They signalled for me to pull over, which never happened with Big

Baba's Renault 11 turbo.

An officer with a double chin approached; he looked for all the world like a pelican wearing glasses. He asked to see the vehicle registration documents, as well as my driving licence. 'What on earth's a youngster like him doing with a car like this?' he must have been thinking, as he scrutinised the car's yellowed registration certificate.

When I pulled down the sunshield to remove the logbook, a small envelope fell out and landed in my lap. Inside was a photo.

Aziz's Farm

It was a Polaroid that dated back a good 20 years and reminded me of a line from Proust: 'The memory of a particular image is but regret for a particular moment.'

The photo had been taken in front of the house belonging to Uncle Aziz, a farmer in Western Algeria and one of Big Baba's relatives. We used to love going over there. It meant escaping the hustle and bustle of Algiers and experiencing first-hand a hostile kind of nature.

Walking barefoot over the feverish midday ground and scraping the soles of our feet on tiny stones. Catching locusts only to release them again because we didn't know what else to do. Black cockroaches like leather, their bodies so long that Mina made up a name for them: limousine cockroaches.

Uncle Aziz took us to harvest Barbary figs, with the help of a bamboo pole whose tip was cut in three to make a pincer that hooked the fruit. We used to collect them by the bucketful. But no matter how careful we were, by the end of the day, our hands were always covered in prickles, which Mama Latifa, Aziz's wife, would pull out using her teeth. Her method was rustic but efficient. She would spit the prickles into a small dish.

The house was surrounded by the huge cactus plants that produced these Barbary figs. We called them 'barbed wire figs'.

High up in the mountains the moon was very white, round and full. We could almost touch it. As for the stars, I'd never counted as many in Nice. In the West, far from Algiers, they glowed as far as the eye could see.

After the summer downpours, we would go snail collecting and, at the end of the afternoon, the women would busy themselves with cooking inside the mechta. The aroma of grilled almonds filled the traditional stone house. Mama Latifa baked rye bread while I crouched down next to her, watching her knead the dough. She had been born with half a finger missing, and her husband would often tease her on the subject: 'If I'd known you were half a finger down when I married you, I'd have knocked 2000 dinars off your bride price!'

On Aziz's farm, the boys ran through the fields pushing an old bicycle wheel with a branch; they built tiny windmills using the coloured plastic from powdered milk pouches; they climbed trees and whistled at stray dogs. The little girls wore ribbons in their hair, or brightly coloured headscarves with their thick brown plaits sticking out. I remember the partially sighted old man who used to take his daily siesta in the shade of an almond tree, his bony body lying on an empty wheat sack, his face protected by the large hood of his djellaba. He must be long dead now.

There were rabbits, crammed into cages. As well as oxen, sheep, goats and a few sad mules tethered to the tree trunks.

I recognised the spot instantly because we would often visit it with my family, but when this photo was taken, I was just a chubby-cheeked baby in Big Baba's arms. My two sisters were dressed in identical matching outfits.

My mother used to treat them as if they were twins, despite their age gap. Sometimes, Dounia would try to differentiate herself by unpicking her lace collar or tearing the ribbons off her dress. My mother flew into a rage as soon as she noticed, her high-pitched voice bouncing off the ceiling and crashing down on Dounia's head like a pétanque ball. Every sentence began with: 'Look at your sister, she's not...'

One day, down by the oued where a trickle of water still ran, Dounia had caught an enormous toad. For no reason, she threw it at Mina who was juggling walnuts in the courtyard. By way of punishment, Dounia had come in for a rare hiding, and we nicknamed her alSahira: 'the witch'. My mother kept her apart from Mina for several days and sent her to bed without any supper for several nights.

'She's so jealous, she'll end up doing something really bad to Mina!' people remarked of my big sister.

One year, the whole family was in Algiers for the engagement party that was being held in honour of my mother's youngest sister, Asma. The women in the room wore flashy outfits and jewels, they laughed loudly and fanned themselves with paper plates. Every summer there was one particular style of dress or fabric in fashion, and, for reasons that escape me, the fabric would be named after a television series or character.

That year it was *Dynasty*, the following summer it was the turn of *Knots Landing*. I can even remember a fabric named *Boudiaf*, after an assassinated Algerian president. It's each to their own, when it comes to repurposing world events.

My aunt Asma sat in the middle of the room, on a chair that was covered in golden cloth and wrapped with a big ribbon. On either side of her stood two little girls in almond-green satin dresses. Following tradition, each had to hold a tall candle while the henna circle was applied to the palms of the bride-to-be, and they were under strict instructions not to let their candle go out; this was a task of the utmost importance, to be undertaken with great solemnity.

Everyone was busy admiring the little girls, who had been dressed so elegantly in beautiful clothes bought in France (made in China, of course, but who was telling?)

My sisters looked like two dolls.

In all the bustle of the party, nobody noticed Dounia setting fire to Mina's hair with her engagement candle. Not long after, Asma's mother-in-law said, 'I can smell bouzelouf!'

Bouzelouf is sheep's head roasted over the fire until all the wool is scorched; then you scrape off the wool with a knife, before boiling up the meat and stewing it with chickpeas. My favourite part was the brain. I used to think it made you clever, until the day one of my cousins said, 'If you eat sheep's brain, you'll become as stupid as a sheep. And when you go back to France, they'll put you in prison for leaving a trail of millions of little black droppings behind you wherever you go!'

I stopped eating brain on the spot.

My mother grabbed the candle off Dounia in a fit of rage. Meanwhile, some of the younger women put out the flames in Mina's singed clump of hair. My younger sister was sobbing and scarlet.

The bride remained as stony-faced as all the brides I've ever seen in Algeria. A few women were whispering amongst themselves, 'Those immigrant children have been so badly brought up!'

Outside in the courtyard, Dounia came in for a proper hiding, one so severe that she wet herself. My mother was letting her have it, because of the shame, I guess. The sound of plastic sandals against my sister's skin rang out along the corridor.

A few minutes later, a strange-looking Dounia returned to the main room and started dancing again, as if nothing had happened. Except that her legs were streaming with urine. A hunchbacked old woman dragged her outside by the puff-sleeve of her pretty princess dress, which was now displaying wet patches. 'Go and wash yourself, then change your clothes!' she instructed Dounia. 'You're a disgrace!'

It was with a heavy heart that my mother had to cut Mina's hair. For months after that episode, my sister wore a hideous bob, short on the neck, with her dry frizzy curls rising up to the sky.

After Dounia's big departure, my mother gave up hiding her heartbreak, and took instead to saying, 'In any case, she's crazy! I can't believe she came out of my womb! Do you remember, Mina? She tried to burn you alive at your Aunt Asma's wedding!' Or, 'I knew I could never trust a girl who threw a toad in her own sister's face!'

I tucked the photo into my jacket pocket and drove home in the Renault 11 Turbo, thinking: 'It's crazy how the same memory must be so different for each person'.

Leaving

I had gone to pay Big Baba one last visit before leaving for Paris. His stroke had shaken him so badly, I wasn't even sure if he remembered about my new job. When I mentioned it, he just nodded and pouted with his lower lip.

As I paced the corridors of the neuro rehab unit in search of a doctor, my trainers squeaking on the freshly-polished floor, I found myself wondering once again: 'Is there a lecture given to medical students by an eminent professor on *The Art of Avoiding Patients' Families?'*

Because they seem pretty skilled at it.

I eventually tracked down Doctor 'Catch-Me-If-You-Can' and we talked as we walked.

'Look, with your dad, we're aiming to maximise his potential. We want the best of what's achievable, but we can only speculate.'

I was struck by his turn of phrase: We Can Only Speculate. It sounded like the title of a future Goncourt-prize-winning novel.

'You have to understand that, at his age, the chances of regaining full independence are slim. It's unlikely that he'll recover the same physical abilities as before. What matters is that he's making progress, in small but encouraging ways.'

The only word I held onto was 'encouraging'.

I knew I wouldn't be back before November. In the

meantime, Big Baba had given me some advice.

'Eat properly. Say your prayers. Don't make too many friends. One or two is enough. And telephone your mother.'

He had offered the same advice, almost word for word, after finally agreeing to let me go on a school skiing trip to the Alps, aged 11. In the end my parents had no choice, thanks to the insistence of my teacher, Monsieur Mounier.

'Madame Chennoun, if Mourad doesn't come with us, he'll be the only Year 6 student left in Nice! He'll spend three weeks kicking his heels with the Year 5s. When we get back, it'll be even worse. His classmates will enjoy talking about an experience they've shared without him. He'll feel left out!'

'Let me tell you something, Monsieur-the-teacher, everybody feels left out at some point in life. It's got to start one day. This will be character-building for him.'

'If you're worried about the safety aspect, I quite understand. I'm the father of three children myself, but we can't keep them at home for the rest of their lives. They have to learn to grow up and spread their wings. I give you my word that the team will keep a close eye on everything.'

'And what about that coach accident in the tunnel, back in November? Those children were only eight years old! Did you see it on the television? Dead, every single one of them! They were on their way to the mountains too, and for all I know their teacher gave his word to their parents!'

'Accidents can happen anywhere, Madame Chennoun. Your son might fall over and injure himself right here, in your garden!'

'Yes, well, that garden's due for a tidy-up, isn't it, eh, Abdelkader? My husband will get rid of all his scrap metal! It'll be less dangerous with just the grass and flowers. And another thing, you don't get avalanches in the back garden.

I don't want him falling into some ravine – my son's never been skiing before!'

'Like most of the children in my class...'

'Back home, Monsieur-the-teacher, nobody gives a fig about snow. People don't ski in Algeria!'

'Well, Mourad is lucky enough to live in France where he can learn.'

'Lucky enough to live in France? Lucky my foot, pfff!'

The way she had said it, there were at least ten kilos of irony on the scales, and keep the change, Monsieur-the-teacher!

Big Baba glowered at her before muttering in Arabic: 'I've never known anyone so stubborn...'

Nobody could outdo my mother when it came to repartee, but my teacher knew that he'd wear her down in the end. As for Big Baba, he was keeping quiet, busy figuring it out. A vein bulged on his forehead, a sure sign that things were simmering inside. He had put on a suit to welcome my teacher, and naturally he'd clipped his regulation Bic biros into his jacket pocket.

He had shown my class teacher into the house with the words, 'Yours is a noble profession, Monsieur!'

I remember watching the scene through the curtain of the girls' bedroom, which gave onto the living room. I was a bundle of nerves and my hands were clammy.

'In any case, Mourad doesn't want to go. He needs his routine. I know he'll be unhappy over there in those mountains!'

'What if we put the question to him directly, Madame Chennoun?'

I clenched my fists. My nails dug so hard into my palms they left marks behind.

Big Baba called me in and invited me to sit on a chair.

Each time we received a guest at home, which wasn't very

often, my mother made mint tea. She arranged pretty lace doilies on the table and laid out bowls heaped with almonds, pistachios, peanuts, and savoury nibbles.

I resisted the urge to grab a handful of them and chew noisily to avoid what was coming next.

'So, Mourad, what do you think about all of this? Tell us, would you rather join the rest of your class on our trip to the mountains, or would you prefer to stay at home and spend two weeks with Madame Bisset's Year 5 class?'

'I don't know...'

'My son, do you really want to go all that way in the cold and, who knows, you could fall and end up dead in an avalanche, or would you prefer to stay with us, and Maman will buy you that gaming console you've been asking for?'

My mother had no issues with blatantly bribing her children.

'I don't know... Both.'

'What do you mean, both? You can't multiply yourself and be in two places at the same time! My son, you have to choose!'

I looked into Big Baba's eyes for help. He must have seen the distress in mine.

'That's enough. He's going.'

'What do you mean, he's going?'

'You heard me, he's going, he's a big boy now. He needs to learn to fend for himself, the teacher's right. You won't be by his side forever to blow on his hot milk or cut up his steak!'

My father has always adopted a pragmatic approach. He keeps quiet, unless he's making a pronouncement. What he said that day was a liberation for me.

'Is it true, Mourad, that you want to go?'

'Yes, Maman. I'd like to go.'

I fiddled nervously with the doily to avoid looking at her.

'I'm going to get a glass of water!' she declared, leaping to her feet. 'Quick a glass of water! My poor heart will stop!'

A cold handshake took place between my mother and Monsieur Mounier. From then on, she considered him a child-snatcher. For several days, the face she pulled was so long it stretched half-way down the street. She felt betrayed, both by Big Baba and by me.

A few weeks later, she burst into tears while packing my suitcase.

On the day I was setting off on the trip, Big Baba dropped me in front of the school. He had made my mother stay at home. I think he wanted to avoid a scene. I wouldn't have put it past her to hang on to the back of the coach for several metres, shouting, 'Give me back my baby!'

While Monsieur Mounier was busy counting the children, Big Baba gave me a kiss and said, 'Be sensible. Eat properly. Say your prayers. Don't make too many friends. One or two is enough. And telephone your mother.'

I had a lump in my throat as I left the hospital. A small mean voice inside my head whispered: 'Imagine that's the last time you'll see him.' But I tried to get rid of it.

I trudged back into the house with a sense of having abandoned my father. My mother had ironed, folded and packed my clothes in my suitcase. The same one I'd used for the school trip to the mountains when I was 11. She had also done copious amounts of cooking, the results of which she'd wrapped in foil for the journey. Food, lots of food. Same as always.

'Maman! I'm not travelling from Nice to Paris by camel! I don't need all this, you know! You've made enough for an army!'

'God forgive me, but why do I have such ungrateful

children?! Mourad, you're going to kill me! Couldn't you simply say, "thank you"?'

'Thank you, Maman!'

'I went to a great deal of trouble!'

'I know, Maman, I'm sorry. Thank you very much!'

'A little recognition wouldn't come amiss! We break our backs and what do we get for it? Criticism!'

'Thanks, Maman, you're the best mum in the whole wide world!'

'And now you're making fun of me, eh...? Stop teasing me! Tfffou!'

I kissed her on the forehead and she smiled. Her sense of sacrifice weighs me down, but it amazes me too. Then she burst into tears. Again.

'Come on, Maman, cheer up!' said Mina, laughing and hugging her. 'Your son has grown up! He's a man now, he's not a baby any more!'

'You're laughing because you don't understand what I'm feeling!'

'Oh yes I do, I've got children too, remember, so of course I understand!'

'It's not the same! My God! El kebda, el kebda!'

El kebda literally means liver, as in the organ. Symbolically, it represents a mother's attachment to her children.

I imagine my mother's liver to be bloody and tender. I worry I'll never love as much as she does.

'Allah commanded us to honour our parents! And the mother in particular! Do you see my foot? Well, paradise lies below it for you! And that's a promise from God!'

We need at least the prospect of paradise to survive this world down below with a glimmer of hope. Promises from God are the only ones I believe in.

Paris

It was the first time I was catching a plane to anywhere that wasn't Algiers, and I felt underwhelmed. I'm sure plenty of people would have been deliriously happy in my place; 12A, window seat, about to take off for the most beautiful city in the world.

I ate a tuna brik made with love by my devoted mother while counting my blessings that I wasn't spending €5.90 on a vegetarian club sandwich. When it comes to low-budget airlines, there's nothing included in the price – apart from the ticket.

I tried to relax as a lanky air steward demonstrated the safety procedures. In his head, he was already giving it his all on Broadway or wherever. He pulled on the cords of his safety jacket rather flamboyantly for my tastes. Given the instructions only apply in the event of an imminent crash, I'm not sure I can see panicked passengers slipping on their life jackets as elegantly as that before nosediving into a cornfield.

Not that anyone listens to the instructions anyway.

Sitting to my right, aisle-side, was a girl who looked no more than 20. There was an empty seat between us.

'Excuse me!' she said, just before take-off, 'Seeing as, like, no one's sitting in the middle, can I put my jacket and handbag there? You wouldn't mind would ya?'

I didn't mind. Or not yet.

She was chewing gum noisily and blowing large bubbles, which she popped with the tip of her tongue.

Her outfit was self-conscious: diamante encrusted everything, bright red nails and lips, too blond, lots of lace and frills. I didn't say vulgar. Or not yet.

'Whatcha reading?'

I was trying to re-read *The Grapes of Wrath*, and I wasn't keen on this conversation opener. I go by the motto: 'if my book is open, your mouth is closed'.

'Er... It's the story of a family in exile in the United States in the Thirties...'

'Is it? I like reading too. I'm more into magazines, though. I read all of them: *Voici, Oops, Closer, Public, Shock, Interview*. It's nice to know what's going on, yeah...?'

'...'

'You're not much of a chatterbox, are ya? D'you want some gum?'

'That's kind, but no thanks...'

'I'll be honest, yeah – I always say what I think – you should take one; it stinks of tuna 'round here.'

'Ah... Sorry.'

'Go on! They're sugar-free.'

'Thanks.'

'What are you planning on doing in Paris, then?'

'I'll be working there.'

'Oh yeah? As what?'

'I'm a newly qualified teacher. It's my first posting.'

'I bet you're a French teacher!'

'That's right.'

'I mean, it's not hard to guess, seeing as you're holding a book! School was, like, so not my thing!'

Not her thing. Am I surprised?

'Relaaaaax. You're well uptight. It's all good, I'm not tryna flirt with you. You're not my type. I'm not into eggheads, such a snooze-fest. And I don't go for chubby guys either.'

Chubby? Me? I'm starting to feel annoyed here. But I'm too polite to bury myself in my book again and ignore her silly peroxide remarks.

'Right... fine. Well, at least that's clear. And what are you going to be doing in Paris?'

'You won't even believe this, but, like, you might be sitting next to a future celeb! No lie, I auditioned for *Betrayal Season 5* and I've got a recall! I'm dying, I'm just so pumped. Going on telly! Being famous! It's beyond unreal, it's been my dream for like forever!'

Without wanting to judge her, some people have microscopic dreams.

'The first programme in the new series goes out live on TF1 next week! Can you believe it?!'

'I'm sorry, you're going to think I'm a bit of an 'egghead' here, but what is *Betrayal*?'

'Are you being serious?'

She burst out laughing and it sounded like a tube of confetti going pop.

'Yes, I'm serious!'

'Oh em gee, *what*? Like, what? What rock have you been living under? Have you not got a TV or something?'

I wish I'd had the nerve to explain a few things to her.

Listen close, blondie, though what I'm about to say may reverberate inside the hollow space between your ears until you can't sleep at night. It may echo louder than a mountaineer shouting on the rooftop of the world: 'Ha-llooo, is there anybody out there?'

You'll never understand my universe! It runs parallel to yours, no, make that perpendicular. Don't you fret, we do have a telly, but our telly is tuned 24/7 to Nilesat, and the news reads at the bottom the screen from right to left. And as for your stories of 'Betrayal', well, there's enough of it in real life! So what do you say to that, you half-baked sex-shop mannequin?

'But yeah, definitely your future students are gonna know it! Basically, it's a TV show, all the contestants live in a house together for 16 weeks, and then everyone's divided into two groups: the betrayers and the betrayed. In each group, there's a leader who's like the strategic master, and each week the public votes for one of the groups. You can win the jackpot of 200 grand plus there's personal cash prizes and stuff... If I do well, I could pay off my mum's debts. She's not even sure she'll live to clear them, poor thing, she has breast cancer and that, and it's all mad scary!'

I felt a fool. I'd jumped to hasty conclusions about the poor girl.

'Cos back in her day, women took off their bras and, like, burned them. Now she's 50, she's practically never had proper support for her boobs so obvs she only goes and gets a stupid tumour. When I saw the mammogram, I almost screamed. It was like she had a ping-pong ball right in the middle here! I'm planning to speak about it live on camera cos the prod team told me it'd, like, totally swing the points my way.'

Then again, maybe not. My judgement was less wide-of-the-mark than I'd feared.

The expression 'selling your own grandmother' sprang to mind.

She didn't stop jabbering in my ears, which were already buzzing from the air pressure. *Can silicone resist altitude*? I wondered, as I stared at her.

Trouble was, I couldn't bring myself to interrupt her in full flow. That's my upbringing for you: we never get over it.

My mother used to have a friend called Gisèle who did door-to-door sales to pay the bills at the end of the month. After her husband died, she would go everywhere with her Tupperware boxes and frying pans. Each time she bumped into my mother in the street, or in the mini-market, she would waylay her for hours. If she wasn't complaining about her meagre pension, she was trying to offload the Tupperware and saucepans. Mina, who doesn't mince her words, encouraged my mother to give Gisèle the cold shoulder.

'Maman, I was beside myself with worry! Where were you?'

'I ran into Gisèle...'

'Is your wheelie-bag empty? Look, this is beyond a joke! You went out to do your shopping at the market and you've come back with an empty wheelie-bag?'

'By the time I'd finally got there, all the stallholders had packed up. There was just the Chinese man selling lighters.'

'Gisèle's out of order! You've got to tell her, Maman!'

'The poor woman lives all by herself, she's needs someone to talk to.'

'Fine, let her talk to someone, but someone...else!'

'Meskina, I feel sorry for her. It's not easy for her.'

'Come on, you've listened to her for hours on end, you've bought millions of saucepans and plastic boxes from her! The kitchen cupboard's full to overflowing!'

'You don't know what it feels like to grow old alone!'

'Nor do you!'

My mother's criteria for taking pity on people were random and subject to change.

One day, she might say about the Roma, 'Look at those gypsies! They beg in the cold with their babies! It's scandalous. Some of them even chop off their arms for the money! Tfffou!'

And the next day, 'The citizens of Nice have no heart! Those poor travellers are driven out wherever they go! If only someone would give them a job, they wouldn't have to ask for money in the streets!'

But my mother is also a very generous woman, who reflects the spread she lavishes on her own table.

She's always said, 'Those who eat well have warm hearts!'

When it came to the July ritual of our holidays to Algeria, we always ended up with excess baggage, despite the 30-kilo luggage allowance. Every year, my mother would cart along a tonne of presents and then put on a show of surprise at the weigh-in.

'Yéééé, 13 kilos excess? I don't believe it! There's something wrong with your scales! That can't be right! My suitcases weren't over when I weighed them at home!'

'Madame, your suitcases are so heavy you could have put a corpse in there.'

'So, you like to make jokes, my son, that's a good sign. Tell me... you're Algerian, aren't you?'

'No, Madame, I'm French...'

'Are you sure you don't have Berber ancestors? You look Kabyle to me.'

'This isn't the first time someone's tried that approach, Madame! And it won't get you out of paying the excess. You need to go to the counter on your right, by the bureau de change.'

'Please, my boy. Look, these are just small presents for the family; skirts, deodorants, underwear...'

'There's nothing I can do about it...'

'Last time, it was a Moroccan girl in your place, and she let our suitcases through without making us pay.'

'That's against the rules, I'm afraid ... I'm *simply obeying orders.*'

'Simply obeying orders, eh? With an attitude like that, I bet members of your family tortured members of my family!'

'I'm being professional, Madame, I'm just doing my job.'

'But it's unkind! Making people pay isn't a job!'

'I'm sorry, Madame. To your right, please.'

'Right? Far right, yes! Racist!'

Anyone who didn't agree with her was automatically a racist.

My father nudged her with his elbow. 'Be quiet! Do you think you're at the fruit and veg stall? Stop haggling. Let's just pay. Why do you put us through the same song and dance every year?'

My mother eventually gave up, adding the habitual 'Tfffou!' under her breath as we headed over to the office to settle our excess baggage bill.

She would spend the whole summer handing out those presents: clothes, bottles of perfume, shoes, and toys for the children. All the items she had managed to stockpile from doing the markets weekend upon weekend, month after month.

Sometimes, when she'd already given everything away, we'd receive a visit from an unexpected guest, prompting her to rush into the bedroom in a panic and grab something from our belongings.

'Maman, have you seen my football shirt?'

'Have another look in the blue suitcase. You're talking about the shirt for the team that loses all its matches, right?'

'Maman, d'you know where my purple dress went?'

'You're sure you didn't leave it behind in Nice? Anyway, it makes you look fat.'

'Where's my striped shirt?'

'Which one, Abdelkader? They're all striped!'

My father gave her a hard time for setting off with suitcases full to bursting and returning home, as he put it, *without a stitch on our backs.*

After we'd touched down in Paris, a television crew appeared at the arrival gates to welcome my neighbour from 12C. The crew comprised a journalist with her sound engineer and cameraman. The aspirational girl from Nice looked instantly at ease when the microphone was thrust in her direction; she was taking her role as a future reality TV star very seriously. Like a discounted Marilyn Monroe showering in the light, she blew kisses to the camera, her acrylic nails narrowly avoiding scratching her nose. Of course, she'd watched her idols do this on repeat. A few curious travellers began to stare and wonder: 'Is she famous?'

I even saw a man trying to take her photo on the sly.

A little further off, I recognised my own personal welcoming committee: a young Algerian who'd emptied a pot of extra-strong-hold hair gel over his head – cousin Miloud.

The Fly in the Coffee

'Havva good trip? Not too tired?'

Miloud's accent was much less pronounced than the last time I'd seen him.

I hardly recognised my cousin. This wasn't the same person I'd left behind in Algiers, the one who got out of bed in the morning and washed his eyes in his own spit.

'Come on, Mourad! The car's over that way!'

Miloud insisted on carrying my suitcase as we crossed the underground car park. Even his physique had changed: he seemed fitter, more muscular. Close-shaven, he gave off a whiff of fruit juice. My cousin was wearing a brand new electric-blue leather jacket and his shoes gleamed under the neon lighting.

'So you think I've changed, eh? Wait! You ain't seen nothin' yet!'

He turned abruptly to face me, flashing a broad smile. 'I got new teeth!'

'Wow! Bsahtek!'

'You'd think they're real, right?'

'Nice work!'

'German dentist, in the 8th arrondissement.'

Of course, I should've spotted them straight off. His teeth!

In his youth, Miloud had hung out on the cafeteria terraces of Algiers. He had acquired a taste for 'presse'; strong coffee served in a tiny tea glass, which he could sip at for hours. A smoker of counterfeit Winstons from the age of ten, alongside his presse he chain-smoked cigarettes, to the point of feeling nauseous. End result: by the time he was 30, he possessed the teeth of a dying camel. Admittedly, he'd always been good-looking, but his new teeth gave him much more bite.

When Miloud took the car key from his pocket and activated the remote unlock, I couldn't hide my astonishment.

'*That's* your car, Miloud?'

'Yep! That's my car! C-Class Merc, SportLine Saloon! J'dida! Fresh from the showroom!'

'Bsahtek! Did you win at EuroMillions, or what?'

'Nearly, cuz. Nearly.'

Still, you couldn't stop Miloud from hanging his prayer beads or road-toll vignette, in the colours of Barcelona FC, from the rear-view mirror.

'Come on, I'm Algerian, you know we'd die for the Spanish league! We can't change our nature!'

As we drove along, I had no idea where my cousin was taking us. But it looked increasingly unlikely that we were headed for the young migrant workers' hostel I'd been expecting.

The shrill female voice from the Sat Nav got straight to the point. *Destination: Home – 17, Rue Michel-Ange, 16th arrondissement, Paris.*

'Make yourself comfortable, cuz.'

'That's not difficult!'

On the comfort-front, this was a far cry from Big Baba's Renault 11 Turbo.

Miloud switched on his state-of-the-art CD player while overtaking every other vehicle on the motorway.

I'd forgotten just how long they went on, the intros to those raï songs. Miloud was invincible when it came to raï. He could have listened to it non-stop, day and night. Given half a chance, he'd have hooked himself up to a drip: raï music direct into his blood stream.

On the day Cheb Hasni was murdered, 18 years ago, Miloud scarifed himself. He also wept for weeks on end and lost loads of weight. Now, whenever he listened to the Cheb's music, he whispered 'Allah y rahmou' before pressing play.

After an intro so long you could be forgiven for forgetting there was a singer involved, I finally recognised the song Miloud was playing. It was a hit by Cheb El Hindi: *Ndiha gawriya.*

The song tells the story of a young man who decides to recover from his disappointment in love by falling for a 'Frenchie' and running away with her. It made a splash in the 90's. Miloud is a purist, specialising in old-skool raï.

'D'you remember?'

'You bet! You used to listen to it on a loop, while chain-smoking.'

'This song is my life! I even listened to it in prison!'

For Miloud, France was a dream.

As a boy, he could never understand why Mina cried at the end of the holidays when it was time to fly back to Nice.

'In your shoes, I'd be crying about coming here at the beginning of July! You don't know how lucky you are!'

'Nor do you!' Mina would sniff.

'So anyway, how's your father?'

'He's doing well, hamdoullah.'

'It's so sad. When I found out what happened to him, it broke my heart! He was so active, right? Always fixing things, always on the move.'

'Right.'

'I pray for his recovery, insha'Allah.

'Thanks, Miloud.'

I had a flashback to the day Miloud stole 1000 dinars from Big Baba's toolbag. He must have been 13 or 14 at the time, and already a seasoned seducer. He used the money to invite girls to an ice-cream parlour called *La Baie d'Alger*. I snitched on him to my uncle, who reacted by hurling a screwdriver at Miloud's head and cracking his skull. 'Forget the money!' my mother kept screaming. 'Don't hurt him! Meskine!' Afterwards, she poured coffee powder on the wound. According to her, it would help it scar and heal over.

I don't know why I suddenly recalled that incident. I found myself staring at the back of Miloud's head, wondering if the scar was still there, but it was impossible to see anything with all that hair gel.

The automatic garage door opened slowly, as Miloud turned up the volume on the CD player.

'Normally, I pump up the music louder – Hasni at top volume to piss them off! But it's not worth it now. No one's around. They've all split for the Côte d'Azur.'

Even if I sold all my bodily organs, it occurred to me while I was admiring the outside of the Haussmann block, *I couldn't pay the rent on a single square metre here.*

I had never seen such a vast apartment, let alone one decorated with so much taste. There were gigantic paintings hanging from the walls. The parquet floor had been polished until it was spotless and its centrepiece was a stunning Persian carpet. My mother would have been beside herself.

I scanned the living room from top to bottom; not a hint of a plastic flower anywhere.

There was lacquered furniture, an enormous dining table, a chandelier *and* a grand piano. Black and so shiny that I could see my reflection in it.

'That's *Liliane* for you. She bought this piano, but she doesn't know how to play.'

To own a piano like that, without playing it, seemed the height of luxury. I was keen to find out more about this Liliane. But I was even more keen to discover why my cousin Miloud could walk all over her Persian carpet.

I could see he was amused by my reactions and relishing the suspense. He couldn't wait for me to interrogate him, and I was about to do so when a tall thin man appeared in the room.

'Good day, messieurs.'

Sporting a trim moustache and a white waistcoat, he looked like a tap-dancer straight out of a black-and-white movie.

He reminded me of the expression 'as straight as a ramrod'.

'Hey, Mario! Wassup, chouïa?'

Miloud turned to me and winked. 'This is Mario, our butler!'

Despite Miloud's enthusiastic introduction, Mario maintained the same frozen expression he had adopted since entering the room.

'Lunch is se*rrr*ved. If you would care to *rrr*elocate to the table.'

Upon delivering his lines, complete with rolled r's, Mario left much as he had entered. Stiff as a poker.

'He's Italian. Liliane brought him over from Milan. He's somethin' else, but he's a nice enough guy. Right, I'm starving. Come on, let's eat!'

'Miloud? When are you going to explain this mix-up?'

'There's no mix-up, just a leg-up, cuz!'

On the menu: cushion of veal, sautéd vegetables and potato

purée à l'ancienne.

I was expecting a television crew to rush in at any moment, clapping. Miloud would be cackling like a madman, showing me where the camera was hidden. He'd have everyone in tears of laughter. And we'd watch ourselves on primetime TV the following Saturday evening.

While my cousin and I were eating lunch, Mario stood against the wall, staring into thin air. I was reminded of school punishments. It made me feel uncomfortable. I hardly dared to eat. I even started worrying: what if poor Mario was hungry? Nobody should be that thin.

Miloud, on the other hand, felt at home. He was mopping up the gravy with big chunks of bread and chewing noisily.

I stared at the mouldings on the ceiling as I sank my fork slowly into the veal.

'Don't you like it, cuz?'

'No, I do, I do. It's really good!'

'Well then, eat! Plus it's halal! I sent Mario to the other side of Paris to find a Muslim butcher! Specially for you!'

I tried not to keep glancing over at that poor, skinny butler with just the one facial expression.

'I'm gonna start at the beginning, otherwise you won't understand a thing! My life's like a film, you get me? You know I had a few problems cos of a girl in Chéraga, and I went to prison? So, no suprises, that story did the rounds of Algiers! A lot of the family turned their backs on me. The girl made the whole thing up! She did it out of revenge! Because I didn't want to marry her! You get me? I'm the innocent party in this story! But you know how it is.... Her dad's brother's a sentencing judge in Algiers, so I stood no chance of being cleared. As for my old man, the chibani's just a poor bus driver. I was lucky to even find a lawyer who'd take on my case. Over there, if you have nothing, you *are* nothing. Hamdoullah, I got a reduced sentence. The day I was let out, my poor mum cooked my favourite dish of grilled peppers.

'After all that, I had to start again from zero. If you could start from below zero, Mourad, that's what I'd have done.... From the basement.'

The trouble is, nobody ever starts again from zero. Not even the Arabs, who invented it, as Big Baba would say.

'I'm telling you, Mourad, my dad barely spoke to me after that. He was ashamed to look me in the eye, and that's what hurt the most! I could read the shame on his forehead, cuz. It's one thing for the law to get it wrong, yeah, but it totally sucks when your own family thinks you're guilty.

'One day, there I was with some friends on the terrace of a cafeteria. We'd ordered two coffees, between the five of us.

'Five unemployed guys. You know that unemployment rate you see in the newspapers? Well, that was us! All five of us representing the stat, '70 percent under the age of 30'.

'I remember that day so clearly, Mourad! One of my friends, Akli, had these Gucci flip-flops, or at least that's what he said they were – he made out they were g-e-n-u-i-n-e Guccis sent by his cousin from Italy! Yeah, sure. Why would Gucci bother making foam flip-flops? So anyway...'

Miloud had taken out a cigarette, and Mario, gliding over the parquet with quick, tiny steps, produced a lighter under my cousin's nose. This butler walked like a geisha.

After inhaling a great big puff of cancer, Miloud carried on.

'We spent the afternoon chatting up skirts on rue Didouche. No luck, cuz. We didn't have a clue. Looking back, we were animals, five bellowing calfs. It was hot, that day. My hair gel was melting down my forehead. We only had 100 dinars left in our pockets. And there was this fly, right, kept buzzing around me. Bugging me so bad, cuz. I kept flicking it away, and it kept coming back, landing on my arms, on my cheek, buzzing around my head. It wouldn't let me go. I even got to wondering; is this a djinn in a fly's body? So I borrowed one of Akli's flip-flops and hit it with a foam sole. Poor thing nose-dived straight into the coffee, like a plane in freefall. I watched it trembling for a few seconds, beating its wings, struggling. It drowned in the end. But it still kept spinning round in the tepid coffee. I mean, it was excruciating to watch, right? So that got me thinking, was I going to end up like that, destined to suffer, to drown after struggling to live a little?'

Miloud kept going with his story for hours. He told me about the racket to obtain a student visa. His arrival in Paris. Dropping out of university. How he'd been put up by a Tunisian garage mechanic. His nights at a club in the banlieue called *Le Saphir Bleu*. The network he'd built up over three years. And finally, the swimming pool at Auteuil. He wasn't wrong when he said his life's a film. By faking his CV, and with the help of a friend, he got taken on as a swimming instructor. He passed himself off as Italian, under the assumed name of 'Tino'.

'Liliane caught on that I was Arab and I think that's what attracted her to me.'

Then again, between a Milanese butler and a waster from Bab el Oued, she must have quickly spotted the difference.

'I was already at the pool, right? So I just had to go fishing! And there were some big fish about, believe me, cuz, with all those ancient floating millionairesses!'

Liliane belonged to the haute bourgeoisie, and to prove it she had a 'de' at the beginning of her surname, bank accounts in

Switzerland, a property portfolio and a sprinkling of Judeo-Christian values. She was the daughter of a famous French jeweller. She had married an ambassador and followed him around the world, going along with his lifestyle and infidelities. Finally, at 50, she had ditched him in Vietnam.

Her only son, Edouard, lived in New York. It saddened her that she saw him so little. He availed himself of her maternal love through bank transfers.

I couldn't *not* put the question to Miloud: 'Do you love Liliane?'

He smiled slyly. 'I like her a lot.'

'That's all?'

'It's a good start.'

'Where is she?'

'She went for coffee with a girlfriend of hers – a journalist or something.'

I was reflecting on how, even though this whole story was kind of far-fetched, it wasn't so surprising, knowing Miloud.

I might even end up getting used to the butler, the silverware, the piano, the king-size bed in the guestroom, the shower with the water massage jet, the gastronomic menus and the incredible view of the Eiffel Tower.

The Phone-call

I had never enjoyed Sundays so much before.

An early riser, Liliane always began by reading the weekend papers. Then, chilled after her half of Xanax, she would join us at the breakfast table where she gave us a recap of what was going on in the world. My cousin liked to down his coffee while stroking his girlfriend's thigh, and I would tuck into a delicious rhubarb brioche. It gave me a warm glow.

On this particular Sunday, after our current affairs, Liliane moved on, once again, to seeking Miloud's opinion about the face-lift she was contemplating. And, once again, his answer came back: 'No way are you tweaking your face!'

'It'll be very subtle. My friend Aude, you know, Charles's wife...? Well she's recommended a surgeon. I can at least meet with him, just to see...'

'No, Liliane. I've said no. Your wrinkles and saggy bits are all part of your beauty.'

'Thanks for the compliment.'

Liliane bit her lip and looked upset.

Or, she did at first.

Then she gazed over at Miloud and kissed him passionately on the lips.

There was something sleazy about their relationship. She enjoyed him dominating her. He had no shame. They both loved people noticing them. I was beginning to get used to it. I didn't ask any questions when they disappeared late at night, mid-week, setting off on foot with a mysterious leather bag.

'What about your father, Mourad? How's he doing?'

Liliane put the question to me after breakfast, just as I was about to leave the table.

The truth of the matter was that the physios kept saying to us, 'He's stagnating, he's depressed, he's lost the will to get better....' But what I told Liliane was, 'He's going from strength to strength!'

'That's great news!' she smiled. 'You know, there's no rush for you to find an apartment-share!'

'Consider this your home!' added Miloud, who was slumped on his chair with an over-full belly.

My cousin considered it to be *his* home, that much was sure. He had probably felt at home from the first moment he set foot inside the apartment.

On the telephone, Mina couldn't believe her ears.

'What a leech! It's disgusting to take advantage of people's weaknesses!'

'Look, she doesn't seem too unhappy.'

'He's a free-loader! As I've always said!'

'I'm telling you, Mina, he's means well.'

'Yeah, right.... Watch out, Mourad. Don't follow him blindly. Don't trust him. And keep looking for somewhere else to live. His decrepit millionairess will grow weary of him one of these days and kick him out. She'll find some other kid who's fresh off the boat, and you'll be in a fix because of that parasite.'

'Don't worry!'

'Anyway, it's not long before the start of term. Make sure you get plenty of rest.'

'Are the children doing well?'

'Yes, very well. Hamdoullah.'

'What about Maman?'

'Oh, you know what she's like. Same as usual. Try to call her more often, please. Every evening, she sobs and kisses your photo. It's creepy.'

'I'll call her right away. Promise!'

'Insha'Allah.'

'And Big Baba?'

'The same. Yesterday, he threw a tantrum at the nurses who wanted to help him put on his made-to-measure orthopaedic shoes. You know what he shouted? 'I'm not wearing boots for cripples!' So Maman just keeps taking couscous to the care team every Friday. She's convinced it's all thanks to her food that they're looking after Papa properly. I'm not joking, he's becoming unbearable!'

Life was carrying on without me. I'd have missed Nice even more if it hadn't been for those delicious rhubarb brioches. And the incredible library. Some of the novels were even signed by the authors. Liliane owned the finest collection of books I'd ever seen. It was almost impossible for me to be bored.

My telephone didn't ring much. So when I felt it vibrating in my jeans pocket, I immediately thought of her.

'Hallo? Mourad?'

And yes, it was Dounia. With her slightly husky voice.

Her photo on the front page of *Nice Matin* flashed up again. Her short hair. Her smoky eyes.

'Hallo?'

'Yes?'

'It's Dounia...'

'...'

'Thanks for calling me back.... You okay?'

'I'm good, and you?'

'Fine, thanks...'

'It's weird hearing you like this. I mean... You sound like a man now.'

'Yeah, well, it's been a while, I guess...'

The last time I'd spoken to Dounia, my voice hadn't finished breaking. Like all 16-year-old boys, I was a hybrid: part-child, part-monkey.

'It's weird for me too, hearing you. I don't know where to start, Dounia.'

'Look, no one's finding this easy, but let's give it a try. It was tough calling you back too, you know. What matters is we're talking now...'

'I'm sorry. I swear, I wouldn't choose to call you in these circumstances. I wish things were different, but here goes. Papa had a stroke a few weeks back and he's in hospital.'

'... You're kidding?'

'No.'

'Shit. Fuck, I wasn't expecting that. Is it serious? What's the damage?'

Her voice quavered, betraying sadness, fear and guilt... A Molotov cocktail of emotions.

'So his right side is paralysed and he has trouble with his memory.'

'But he can still recognise you?'

'Yes, he recognises us.'

'Thank goodness.... I'm grateful to you for letting me know, Mourad.'

'That's okay.'

A long silence followed; heavy, grey and muffled as a

mid-afternoon cloud. The kind of cloud that makes you wonder: 'What are we in for? A sunny spell or a monster thunderstorm?'

'Look, the thing is, he said he wanted to see you.'

'... Seriously?'

'Yes, promise.'

'Papa? He asked to see me? It was his idea?'

'Yes!'

'I find that very surprising.'

'I'm telling you it was his idea.'

If I'd been in Dounia's shoes, I'd have been equally sceptical. Knowing Big Baba, that is. It can be as hard to tease an idea out of his head as it is to get the karakul off it.

'This is bonkers. I don't understand. Why didn't you look me up before? You had to wait until something serious happened. It's so stupid for words. Can you imagine if he hadn't made it...?'

'I know. I've thought about it so many times. But I couldn't see a way. I kept reminding myself you didn't want to see us again. Maman wouldn't have been able to handle it. The way you left us. It was forever.'

'Mourad, you were the little brother, but I always felt close to you. D'you remember?'

'Yes, I felt the same way.'

I thought back to the pair of Stan Smiths that helped me get picked by the captain of the handball team, for the first time in my life.

Before that, I was invisible, always the last kid, staying on the bench while all my classmates heard their names being called out, one by one, to join a team.

There would only be me left, with my cheap tennis shoes, plus this other kid, who was morbidly obese. Aged 12, he weighed 95 kilos and just the idea of warm-up exercises gave him nosebleeds.

'You're not to blame. You were under Maman's dictatorship. So were the other two.'

'No, it wasn't like that! But when you left, she collapsed...'

'Yeah, yeah, panic attacks, high blood pressure... I know.'

Dounia doesn't just think something, she has to say it out loud.

'At first, I was fuming, I'm telling you. When I found out you'd turned up at my workplace, I was beside myself. *They've got some nerve*, I thought. All that time, when nobody bothered to find out how I was doing, and now I've got an important job in the town hall, they send Mourad. I was furious. I was convinced there was a motive. It didn't occur to me there might be this sort of problem.'

'A motive for what, Dounia? Did you think we were after holiday vouchers, or a float at the Nice carnival?'

'Listen, Mourad... there's no point stirring it all up. I'm sorry about Papa. I'm sad to hear this. But I need to think things over. I don't know if I have the strength to forgive.'

I pictured Mina witnessing this conversation. She would be furious, her face bright red with smoke ushering from her ears and nostrils, like in one of those Japanese anime.

'What!!!!' she'd shriek. *'To top it all, she's the one who thinks she needs to find the strength to forgive us???'*

'Mourad, you were too young. You didn't understand what was going on. First they wanted to marry me off, then they wanted me to quit my studies.'

'I never heard anything about any marriage.'

'I couldn't stay and follow the path of mediocrity they'd mapped out for me. I know I must look selfish in your eyes, but the truth is I didn't just leave with a man. I left because of Maman. Pleasing her meant becoming the perfect daughter for her, doing the housework, the dishes, accompanying her every year back to the bled. Naturally, she'd have carried on fattening me up with tajines and almond cakes until, one day, she finally found me a nice devoted little husband who wasn't too picky when it came to appearances. But, deep down, she wanted me by her side forever, she wanted to turn me into a fat, depressed old maid.'

It's crazy. Dounia and I share the same nightmares.

'So what about the skinny guy with the enormous watch?'

'That was my biggest mistake. He was married, but I didn't know it at the time. It's so strange talking about this with you now, when it all seems so long ago. I've started therapy recently with this terrific shrink, recommended by a friend. I see him twice a week. He's awesome.'

I didn't share my opinion on the subject. I loathe shrinks.

'I'm in Paris at the moment as it happens. I have to see my publisher, because my book's coming out in a few days. I've written an account of my personal journey. It's called *The Price of Freedom*.'

I didn't share my opinion about that either. Frankly, it's obscene. It makes it sound like a hostage-freeing story. You'd think Dounia had spent four years in a cave in Afghanistan, or with the FARC in the Colombian jungle. And even then, Íngrid Betancourt still chose a plainer and more understated title for her book. If Maman finds out, let's not even go there with the number of extra medicine boxes to add to her collection.

'I'm a very active campaigner, as it happens, with my organisation. Our message is: *Be who you want to be. Nobody else can decide your future*. I don't know why I'm telling you all this.... Anyway, I'm doing fine, Mourad. I feel calm and serene these days. I'm forging ahead.'

As calm and serene as someone who needs to see a shrink twice a week?

'You said you're in Paris...?'

'Yes, absolutely. I'm here to promote the book, you see, do some radio and newspaper interviews, including the morning show on Europe 1, plus the back page of *Libé.* Get that, the back cover of *Libération*, Mourad! So I can't visit Papa right now. But I'll be heading back to Nice in a few days.'

'I'm in Paris too, that's why...'

'Aha!'

That *Aha!* again.

'So how about we do lunch sometime?'

Dounia's new life involves shrinks and doing lunch.

Aha!

Social Etiquette

Miloud and Liliane had fallen out.

Again.

There'd been a bunch of Liliane's friends over at the apartment for a dinner party: architects, film-makers, policy-makers, artists and an erstwhile guest with a squint, whose job involved organising polo matches in Scotland, or something.

Mario, the butler, stood pinned against the wall, tending to our every wish. He rushed to serve the guests more wine, or water, or bread. Ever-stoical.

Miloud is usually happy to play the handsome toyboy with a tan. He casts sultry looks, in the belief this makes him look 'deep'. When Liliane's intellectual friends have a dig at somebody, he pretends to catch their drift by laughing loudest and seizing the opportunity to show off his new teeth.

On this particular evening, however, the man with the squint, the one who claimed to keep company with aristos and celebrities, wouldn't pipe down. He'd just acquired a vintage British car on behalf of a super-wealthy Qatari, and was bragging about how he was making a killing, thanks to deals like that.

He was a fit-looking 50-something ultra free-market divorcee, with no kids and a serious work ethic about looking laid back. You'd almost have fallen for his relaxed and urbane persona, if the psoriasis visible inside his shirt collar hadn't betrayed his pathological anxiety. Still, Liliane seemed entertained by his boring story.

'Seriously, Lili!' he exclaimed. 'You're telling me you've never taken Milou to Dubai?'

'It's Miloud,' snarled my cousin. 'There's a 'd' at the end. Milou is the name of Tintin's small dog.'

The man with the squint laughed. He turned towards Liliane and said: 'You know what they say about small dogs, Lili? They're faithful. Or, at least they're meant to be...'

Liliane smirked as she sipped her wine. Now it was Miloud's turn to get hot under the collar. His blood was boiling. He was hopping mad.

'Are you calling me a dog?' he asked, standing up and lunging at the man with the squint. 'Say it to my face – tell me I'm a dog, you bastard!'

'It was a joke, for goodness' sake, calm down!'

'Look me in the eye and say it again, like a man!'

'I'm looking you in the eye, for fuck's sake!'

Liliane tried to smoothe things over. But I could tell that she'd never experienced anything as thrilling in her life. She was like a teenager.

'You people are something else, you fly off the handle for nothing!' the man added, adjusting his collar.

Throughout all of this, Mario the butler remained as immoveable as marble, like an Algerian bride.

I dragged Miloud outside.

He started talking in Arabic for the first time since I'd arrived in Paris. I realised that he wasn't so well suited, after all, to being the foil of a rich divorcee with dreams of going under the surgeon's knife.

'He's got no time for bargain basement Arabs like me! He despises me and everything I stand for. If I was an emir's son, he'd have smeared himself like a piece of shit under my big Qatari shoes. Plus, he knows I can't travel to Dubai! I haven't got my papers!'

As for the man with psoriasis, I remember wondering whether his racism was as convergent as his squint.

'Yallah,' said Miloud, 'let's split!'

To my great surprise, Miloud didn't head for the garage when we left the building.

'We're taking the métro!'

It made me think of the film, *My Fair Lady*, in a French-Algerian version. With Miloud in the role of Audrey Hepburn.

Suddenly, his proletariat side was rising up again. He lit a cigarette before dispatching a gob of spit that landed plop in the middle of the pavement.

Miloud stayed quiet. He didn't tell me where he was taking us. Meanwhile, I was discovering the joys of the Paris métro.

A boy in our carriage was using his mobile to film under the skirts of an old woman who had dozed off. And they call it a 'smart' phone? Presumaby, the idiot would post the video on social media and be rewarded with gazillions of Likes.

A little further along, a woman in her forties, dressed to impress, was adding the finishing touches to her make-up. She scowled as she applied her lipstick, and it made her temporarily ugly. I don't know any woman who looks beautiful when she's putting on her lipstick.

'Chat her up!' urged Miloud, reconnecting with his brand new smile. 'You like her, right? Come on, you can't take your eyes off her!'

'Sorry, Miloud, older women aren't my thing.'

'Well, you're into blondes, I've noticed!'

'Not true! Or not especially. No more than brunettes.'

'You're weird, cuz. Apart from books, you're not into

anything! It's like your mind is locked-off.'

'I find everything I need in books.'

'You won't find the laughter of a beautiful girl, or a pair of legs, or the scent of her neck in your books!'

'That's where you're mistaken – there's everything! Look, you go to that Club Med gym where you pay an eye-watering subscription to beef up your biceps on state-of-the-art machines–'

'You know I'm not the one paying, so who cares?'

'That's not the point, Miloud. What I'm trying to say is, for me, reading's a workout, for my imagination and my emotions. If emotions were muscles, I'd be an athlete. Does that make sense?'

He stared hard at me for a moment.

'No.'

I laughed.

'Listen up, I've heard about some kinky shit going down when it comes to the toffs cuz. People getting turned on by shoes, or animals, or leotards or furniture. But I've *never* met someone who gets turned on by books.'

I laughed, level ten.

'If it's because you're a pooftah, I promise not to say anything to your mum. Trust me, I've got this friend, Karim, who lives in Argenteuil and, every now and then, when the raï singers are over giving concerts in the Paris region, he provides them with a bit of company. Sometimes, they're feeling alone in their hotel, they prefer to keep things discreet, a quick phone call to Karim, he hops in his car and heads over. That's just his thing, I don't judge him for it...'

'What's that got to do with anything? I'm like you, I love raï. Not raï singers.'

Miloud's much funnier when he's in the métro, away from the social etiquette of Liliane's dinner table, laid for ten.

Le Saphir Bleu

I'd never set foot in a nightclub before. Let alone a dive-bar for raï music.

In the cobbled recess of a dimly-lit dead-end street, the rain beat down on us. This was the beginning of our night out, banlieue-style.

It felt like we were in some American detective movie.

Definitely not a French one.

French detective movies always start off in the police station, between nine and five, with an overweight detective who's hoarse and in his sixties. In spite of his cholesterol problems, chomping on a sandwich that's jambon-beurre-mayonnaise when a young and inexperienced cop knocks on the office door.

'Superintendent!' he bellows. 'A prostitute's body's been found in the Seine!'

So the detective pulls on his raincoat and takes his sandwich with him, intending to finish it on the way. This is a French film, after all, and that sandwich cost €3.30, so he doesn't want it going to waste. Displaying the kind of vim his chosen career demands, he climbs into an unmarked patrol car. Close-up on the Citroën logo. A tribute to 'made in France'? The detective will lead the inquiry in the next episode.

He jumps every traffic light along the boulevard to reach

the crime scene double-quick, in case the corpse returns to life. On the way, he remembers to call home to check his teenage son is back safely from school and doing his science assignment.

So that's how it is in a French detective film, right? Just thought I'd point out the difference.

As we drew closer to the music, the flashing sign for *Le Saphir Bleu* was in sync with the bass line. Miloud pushed open the swing doors and fell into a long clammy hug with the bouncers.

'Me and them, we're like brothers!'

The two giants had such broad necks you could have drawn the map of the ex-USSR on them.

'When I'm here, I feel like I'm on home turf,' whispered Miloud, letting out a contented sigh.

'Hou là là...' exclaimed the pretty cloakroom attendant, recognising him. 'H'mar mette!'

I love that expression. In Arabic, it's literal meaning is: 'A donkey has died.'

My mother uses it to signal her astonishment at very rare occurrences. For example, whenever my father started sorting the contents of his garage, she would say, 'Yééé, are you tidying your souk? H'mar mette!'

I guess it must have something to do with a donkey's long life expectancy. I once read something about it being at least a third longer than a horse's.

Mademoiselle Cloakroom was called 'Sousou'. A nickname, I was guessing. Miloud kissed her on both cheeks, then the neck. She pushed him away, giggling: 'Buzz off of me!' She had some colourful expressions.

She was reading a celebrity magazine and the girl's face on the front cover looked vaguely familiar. Bam, I managed to situate her: aisle seat, 12C. 'Shock!' ran the headline: 'Cindy comes out about her mother's cancer!' It was on the tip of my tongue to say 'Hey, I know her!'

Inside, people were dancing with outstretched arms, glass in hand. They were laughing and singing as their bodies intertwined. The lighting effects made the club feel like a TV variety show from the eighties. I stood there, soaking up this unfamiliar spectacle.

Some of the men had undone their shirt buttons down to the fourth hole, while the cleavages of the dancing girls were heaving with ten euro notes.

A young DJ kept dedicating songs to absent friends: those who had stayed behind, back in Algeria. He gave shout-outs to families, districts, streets and villages. He seemed to be enjoying himself, to be moved even by these requests.

It occurred to me that, at exactly the same time, those absent friends might also be in a club where they were dedicating songs to *their* absent friends.

I thought of the expression, 'it's always the people who aren't there that get the blame'.

As I watched all those people, I sensed different versions of loneliness. I figured everyone was there to forget something.

Miloud was trying to forget his obsession with that fly drowning in the cold cup of coffee. I was trying to banish the thought of a half-dead father and an octopus-mother who was as loving as she was overbearing.

And all the while, the raï kept flowing.

Deep in his cups, my cousin was holding forth about how American stars owed a big debt to the Algerians.

'Because who d'you think introduced the vocoder into

music, hey?' he spluttered into his glass. 'We did!'

So will Rihanna thank Cheba Djenet for *Matejebdoulich* one day? It's an unsolved mystery.

A small group had formed around two hench guys. One of them, in an over-sized fake-leather jacket, called the other one out for disrespecting him.

'Sit on *that*, asshole!' said the second, giving him the finger.

The guy in the fake-leather flew off his fake-handle, prompting Miloud's two bouncer friends to heave their big necks over to the bar and extricate him without further ado.

'Sami, stop drinking!' they ordered. 'You don't know how to drink!'

I love that expression 'without further ado', by the way, just using it makes me feel happy.

Miloud carried on drinking. Are you supposed to know how to drink? Is there a right way of drinking? So many unanswered questions as I sipped on my fizzy pop. Strawberry-flavoured Ifri. A drink from the old country. A kind of sparkling diabetes.

When they started playing Cheb Hasni's cult track, *Mazal souvenir andi*, my cousin burst into tears. As in, bawling his eyes out like a teenage girl after losing her virginity turned out to be a big letdown. He was inconsolable.

I randomly patted his shoulder, unsure what to do.

Opposite, I noticed a transvestite in a red wig staring at us. He smoked like a man and danced like a woman. If his knees had been less calloused, he would have possessed the perfect pair of legs.

He jerkily rearranged his long synthetic hair and tottered

over to our table on his diamante heels.

'Hey! Stop crying! Pull yourself together! You're a man, for fuck's sake!'

'Look who's talking!'

'It's different!'

'I'm crying because it's hard. This dog's life of ours is so hard.'

'It's hard for everyone! We've all got our shit! I hate it when men cry, it's disgusting. Listen, you're good-looking, you're fit and that jacket you're wearing is worth at least half a grand. So enough with the crying...'

He comforted Miloud with a hug, before opening a small gold handbag and offering him a tissue.

'Come on! You've got a dose of the blues, but it'll pass.'

Then he turned back to his table of girlfriends and poured himself another glass of champagne. He stared at us as he raised his glass, as if to say: 'To your health!'

It was dawn when we left *Le Saphir Bleu*.

We could hear the birds. The sound of birdsong in the small hours always raises my anxiety levels. If I were a musician composing the soundrack for a nightmare, the album would start with birdsong at dawn. *Track 1: Scary Birds*.

Miloud staggered and I helped him as best I could. After a few metres, he wanted to take a leak, which he did, against a wall, saying, 'I piss on every one of you. I piss on all millionnaires. I piss on exile.'

You'd have thought he was reading the epitaph of one of the 'accursed poets'.

We kept switching direction every few minutes. I didn't yet know Paris well enough and Miloud was far too disorientated.

And then time stood still. An old man in white was walking towards us. He wore a chechia and djellaba and was clearly on his way to prayers. He bore an uncanny resemblance to our grandfather, Sidi Ahmed Chennoun. Miloud stared and began to sob.

'What the hell am I doing with my life?'

In the first métro of the morning, a black woman, her forehead pressed against the glass, was staring at her feet. A rosary in one hand, she rolled the small worn wooden beads between the tips of her slender fingers. Given the time of day, I guessed she was a cleaner for some sub-contractor, on her way to clean 15 or so offices before the official working day began. Her face was round and smooth. A beautiful woman who looked as worn as the beads on her rosary.

Back at Liliane's, we both crashed in the guestroom. Miloud passed out cold in the middle of the bed. Even with a drunk man lying across it, the advantage of a king-size is that you've still got enough room to stretch out like a pasha.

Let's Do Lunch

I'd received her text the evening before. *Meet at the Flore, first floor, métro Saint-Germain, 12.30?*

OK, I replied, adding an affectionate *x* but immediately deleting it. I was getting ahead of myself.

Did Dounia arrange all her meetings at *Café de Flore* because of the connection with Simone de Beauvoir? If that was the case, and she'd got some deluded idea about being next in line among feminist icons, then this was going to be awkward.

My nerves were shot, I was suffering from hot flushes and there appeared to be a watermelon in my belly.

On top of feeling apprehensive about our reunion, there was also my sense of guilt. The guilt I still drag around with me. The guilt I'll drag around all my life, like I've got some scrawny bitch on heat following me and sniffing my behind.

I thought of Maman and Mina. What would they say? Was I joining the enemy camp? If they found out, they'd brand me a traitor. I know it may seem counter-intuitive, but acts of betrayal often start with good intentions.

Of course, I arrived early for our meeting. By at least half an hour.

I ordered a Perrier with a slice of lemon, before changing my mind: 'Er, hold on!' The waiter returned to my table. 'Actually, I'll have a café allongé instead...' He looked annoyed. 'Er, sorry, scratch that... I'll have the Perrier, after all...'

He huffed and puffed, turning on his heels again. I felt very foolish.

There were three tourists on the neighbouring table, American girls, judging by their accents. 'Phew,' I thought, 'non-French speakers, so they won't have understood my spat with the grumpy waiter, or figured out how rubbish I am at asserting myself.'

Like all American girls on holiday, they were wearing shorts. Very short shorts, with plenty of flesh on display. White, milky flesh, with skin so delicate you could almost see the blood in their veins. It made you want to pinch them and wait for a bruise to appear.

One of the girls fished a slice of lemon out of her fizzy drink, then gave it to her friend who sank her teeth into it.

I tried to copy her, but the acidity made my gums tingle and I pulled a face like the headlining chimpanzee in a travelling circus.

I was thinking back to my conversation with my mother that morning. I had called home, not about anything in particular, just to find out everyone's news.

'My heart is cracked! It has been torn apart! I thought you were dead! I'm *so* disappointed. Am I not even worthy of a phonecall, in your eyes? Did you know that I go to sleep with your photo? The one of you wearing the blue shirt and your mouth braces... I thought you understood the value of a mother... Do you appreciate what it means to carry a child inside the womb? To feed him from your breast? To watch over him when he has a fever? To worry night and day on his behalf? I am mad! Hopping mad!'

Eight days without phoning = end of the world.

'Sorry, Maman. Forgive me. I was busy here. And it's the first day of term on Monday, so I had to get everything ready.'

Yes, I lied. The truth was, I'd been lounging about. Reading my favourite Russian authors, while lying in my underwear on a scandalously comfortable king-size bed. But now I was scared. Scared she'd rumble me, just from my voice. With her nif, her nose for sniffing things out, her Algerian mother's intuition, I was convinced she'd realise I was plotting with the enemy.

'You're so ungrateful, all of you! Did you know that people who don't behave well towards their mothers never amount to anything? Did you know that? They're cursed!'

'I know, Maman.'

'What's going on? You're acting funny!'

'Nothing, Maman. Everything's fine!'

'Are you sure about that? I can tell you're hiding something from me! I know you, Mourad! Your voice, it's not like normal!'

'And I'm telling you, I'm fine, Maman.'

'Ya Allah, have you slept with a women?! Is that it? Eh? Tell me the truth!'

'Maman!!! No, there's nothing! Stop it!'

'You be careful. I can feel it when something's going on, I can feel it in my womb.'

'So anyway, how's everything? What about Papa? Is he making progress with his neuro rehab?'

'Things don't progress with your father. They go backwards!'

'Why?'

'He's got it into his head that it's all pointless! I visit him in hospital every day God gives us! From noon to nine o'clock at night! I spoon the food right into his mouth. And I wash him, because he refuses to let anyone else do it! As for his rehab, he just tells us: "It's not worth it! I'm too old! It's all over for me!"

'He's so self-centred! The truth is, because of him it's all over for *me*! He moans about everybody. The black nurses insult him in their own language, you know! And if I spoke that language, I'd do exactly the same.'

'What about the doctors? What do they have to say?'

'Tfffou, doctors! Tfffou! Why do they even bother with ten years of studies, eh? I bring them cakes, I bring them couscous, and what do they say to me? "Your husband doesn't want to fight. We can't do the work for him. He has to want it for himself!" I've seen the exercises they do, and they're rubbish! They make him shell pistachio nuts and pick up coins. He barely moves his fingers.'

'It's called occupational therapy, Maman, it's for his fine motor skills.'

'Do you want to hear the best? Now, when he's annoyed, he says to me: "The thing is, everyone will be happy when I'm dead!" Can you imagine? Yesterday, he said, "Djamila, throw me out of the window!" So what was my answer? "Even for that, you need me!"'

'You're still holding things together, though?'

'If I don't hold them together, who will? Eh? A son who phones me once a year? Let me tell you, my morale is at zero, zero, zero. Any other woman in my shoes would have packed her bags and headed for Algeria, without a backwards glance.... But I'm doing my duty. And it is my duty.'

Of course Maman's very dedicated. She always has been. And she's making a big deal out of it too. She always does. That doesn't bother me. What's terrifying is that she expects as much back.

Clearly, it wasn't the moment to tell her that I was about to see my sister again.

A week without a call from me and she was already grievously wounded, so I hardly dared imagine how she'd react. 'By the way, Maman, I'm having lunch with Dounia at midday and I bet she's going to badmouth you for hours behind your back.'

Come to think about it, Big Baba isn't the only one who might benefit from re-habilitation. Our whole family could do with some re-education: back to basics, picking up coins and shelling pistachios in our heads. Group therapy. Starting again from zero. Except it's always the same refrain, nobody starts again from zero, not even the Arabs who invented it, as Big Baba would say.

Dounia walked into the café. She was on her phone and glancing around, so I waved my right hand which was horribly clammy. She saw me and ended her call. I stood up. I was tense and as stiff as Mario.

I won't lie, it was very emotional. I was on the verge of tears, but Big Baba said men don't cry, and the transvestite in *Le Saphir Bleu*, the one with the red wig, went further, saying it's disgusting when men cry.

It was weird seeing Dounia walking towards me. I stared at her. She looked thin.

She placed her handbag carefully on the chair, hesitated, then threw herself at me. 'Oh my God...Mourad!' she kept saying, as she hugged me tight. She smelled of fruits-of-the-forest yoghurt. We stood there, staring at each other for the longest time.

The Americans were shooting us discreet looks. Well, discretion, Midwest-style.

'Oooh cuuuute!' said one of them, wrinkling her nose.

They must have thought it was a lovers' tryst. Hello, team blonde shorts, you couldn't be wider of the mark. There's a whole other story playing out here.

Same as the last time I'd seen her, there were tears in Dounia's eyes as she opened her handbag. She was rummaging around for something. And it was taking forever.

'Nice handbag,' I said, to break the spell of feeling awkward.

'Really? You like it? It's from the new Balenciaga collection.'

What could I add to that?

'Here you go!' she announced, finally producing a book from her luxury accessory and holding it out. 'This is your copy. I've written inside it for you, but please don't read my dedication now, it'd be embarrassing...'

I had a quick flick-through and glanced at her photo on the cover. A beautiful portrait of Dounia. Her face looked less gaunt. The text on the promotional wrap-around band read: Director of the charity *Speak Out Sister*!

'I hope you'll find time to read it. You'll give me your honest opinion, right?'

Not on my life.

'Of course!'

The grumpy waiter returned to our table. He inquired very politely of Dounia what she'd like to drink. He was pulling out all the stops, with my sister and her little linen dress.

Dounia ordered a diet drink. To match her bag and dress.

In half an hour, I'd had plenty of time to down my glass. Not a single ice cube remained. Everything had melted.

'So, are you coming to see Papa?'

It wasn't like I had any convincing arguments up my sleeves. I just sat there, arms splayed, elbows on the table, sucking through a straw.

'Seeing Papa means seeing Maman and Mina again.'

The Americans were heading off now. No doubt for a spot

of shopping on the boulevard Saint-Germain.

I stared idiotically at Dounia, willing her to agree. I felt like a job applicant at their first interview: limited qualifications, zilch experience, nothing to offer. The kind of candidate who's hoping for a charm offensive. Except they answer in monosyllables – yes, no – and they're so transparent you can see right through them. The kind of candidate who writes *films, reading, travel* under 'Interests' at the end of their CV.

If I'd been interviewing me, I'd have extended a limp handshake and said, 'We'll let you know!'

'Mourad, you should pay more attention to your posture,' Dounia rebuked me. 'You'll end up with scoliosis!'

So I sat bolt upright. 'Sir, yes sir!' I nearly answered.

Military service is no longer compulsory in France, thank God. But if it were, my mother would have devised a cunning get-out plan, which would probably have involved getting me psychologically classified.

Speaking of which, that was why Miloud enrolled at a university in Paris: to escape national service in Algeria. He was granted an exemption. 'It wasn't so much a brain drain,' he confided, 'as a case of cowards splitting!'

Dounia bucked my expectations by ordering not warm goat's cheese salad but steak tartare.

Eating steak tartare? I'll eat my hat if that's not true integration for you.

Because learning a language, respecting state institutions, embracing a country's culture by cherishing its great writers, marching for the glory of the nation... all that counts for nothing compared to stuffing your face with raw chopped steak splatted with egg yolk and some condiments.

Culture clash.

Suddenly, I'm picturing Uncle Aziz, sitting at table with us.

The reckless farmer who still takes pride in wearing his rezza, the traditional yellow turban he wraps around his head. The man who whispers in his sheeps's ears before slitting their throats. Or who only has to spit out a fruit stone to make a tree grow.

'Look, uncle, this plate of raw meat costs €27. That's about 2800 dinars!'

I can picture him shaking his head in bewilderment: 'Tfffou!'

Yes, no question about it, an appreciation of this expensive gastronomical muck represents an enormous step towards integration.

I have to admit that it was with a certain amount of disgust I watched Dounia masticating her raw meat. I couldn't help but think of the anonymous *homo erectus*, thanks to whom we owe the discovery of fire some 400,000 years before Jesus Christ. Dounia wasn't doing him justice.

I communicated our family news over the course of our meal. Or, at least, the bits I thought were essential.

Dounia freaked out when she learned that Mina was married with three kids. Her eyes were as wide as those of a presidential candidate just before the results are announced.

'What can I say? I feel so uncomfortable with these pre-ordained paths. Why lead a monumentally dull life, walking in Maman's footsteps? Working at the care home, marrying a blédard...'

'Who said he was from the home country? He was born here, just like us! Plus, Jalil's a super nice guy.'

'Yeah? I hope he's not some kind of fanatic who'll keep her stuck at home, force her to wear the veil, Macho & Co!'

'Not at all! Stop it! Where's all this coming from? You know as well as I do that nobody can force Mina to do anything.'

I felt like emptying that plate of raw chopped meat into her handbag. Was I developing a new obsession?

'What can I say...? Personally, I couldn't do it.'

'Couldn't do what?'

'Be in a relationship with a guy... who was just like me. Someone too similar to me.'

'Jalil isn't similar to Mina just because he happens to be an Arab. Take you, you're her own sister and you two are complete opposites.'

'That's got nothing to do with it. I mean, he's given her three kids! Settling down with a guy who shares the same heritage as you, the same references, the same codes, the same upbringing, well, you're missing out on a lot of enrichment as a couple.'

'Or not. You might be missing out on a lot of hassle.'

I was thinking of Miloud and Liliane, who are hardly a role-model couple.

In any event, if slamming the door in your parents' faces and cutting off from your roots led to 'enrichment', we'd have known about it , and that's for sure. For now, all I could see was that it led to cannibalism.

We were both feeling a bit awkward after that conversation and Dounia, who's a smart woman, despite her convictions and the caper caught between her teeth, sensed this.

'Anyway, it's not like I'm in a position to tell anyone what to do.... At 36, I'm unmarried and I don't have any kids! Back in the bled, they'd have thrown me on the rubbish heap, at my age!'

A deep sadness entered her gaze, framed by her smoky eyeliner.

I felt sorry for my big sister.

'What about you, Mourad? Are you with someone?'

'Me? Er... no...I'm not with anybody.'

'Really? How come? You haven't turned out so badly!'

I blushed.

'I haven't got the headspace for it. I work a lot.'

'Working never stopped people falling in love!'

She pulled out her gold bank card which she waved between two skinny fingers in the waiter's direction. Like any self-respecting career woman, she settled the bill while listening to her messages, her Blackberry wedged between ear and shoulder.

We hugged at length, but I felt as if I were holding a stranger in my arms. A stranger who smelled of fruits-of-the-forest yoghurt.

'I don't think I'm up for going by myself. I'd like us to go together.'

So we agreed to make a date in two months' time, during the next school holidays. That way, I'd have a chance to do some groundwork.

'Don't forget to call me when you've read the book!' she added.

I walked her to a taxi rank, where she stepped straight into a black Skoda at the front of the queue.

'See you soon, li'l brother!' she smiled, giving me her famous wink. She had reinstated a sort of complicity between us. It was like daytime drama on Dubai TV.

Blood ties, hey?

Back to School

Miloud and Liliane had made up.

Again.

They spent a week away from Paris to 're-connect' and 'check in' on their relationship. A suite at the Royal Barrière in Deauville, some luxury treatments at the hotel spa and they were ready to start over – fresh as '55, the year Liliane was born.

Since returning, they were like teenagers glued to one another. And Miloud had finally agreed to Liliane undergoing a *gentle* facelift, care of the reputable surgeon her girlfriends had been hotly recommending for months.

Out of curiosity, I typed 'facelift' into YouTube and landed on a gruesome video uploaded by a Spanish surgeon. He stretched his patient's cheek so taut he could have used it as clingfilm to wrap his leftover tortilla.

He started cutting in a straight line using a pair of golden scissors. A strip of skin, two centimetres wide, fell to the tiled floor like a piece of tagliatelle *al dente*. Next, close to the ear, he stitched a hem worthy of a Sri Lankan seamstress. Everything was visible beneath the skin. The Spanish surgeon had scalped this poor woman as if he were a free-market Sioux chieftain.

In the background of the operating room, *I Just Called To Say I Love You* by Stevie Wonder was playing. Bleak.

I felt the same as when I walked past the horse butcher's near our house, in Nice. There are some things you should never see.

That morning, I had risen before dawn. Mario was already up.

It doesn't matter what time you wake, Mario is always up. I don't think he ever sleeps. He's a robot. No emotions, no signs of fatigue, no opinions. He glides, wafting about this outsize apartment like a ghost. There's never a crease on his shirt. He never frowns. Or smiles. And you won't hear him cough or sneeze.

It's a mystery to me. Not even Liliane knows anything about him, and she's been his boss for several years. She found it odd when I questioned her on the subject. Perhaps one isn't supposed to show any interest in the lives of domestic staff?

I had been on the toilet for nearly an hour, praying for the Immodium to take effect. My head kept overheating and I was writhing like a worm. Or a deposed king struggling to leave his throne.

I couldn't swallow any of the stylish breakfast that had been carefully prepared by Mario.

My thoughts turned to my mother. I missed her, perhaps for the first time since coming to Paris. A comforting word from her, a token of encouragement, anything would have been welcome.

Commuting to school meant travelling from Liliane's, near the Arc de Triomphe, out to Montreuil in the banlieue. Using the journey planner on the RATP website, I'd mapped my route via public transport. I printed my itinerary, tucked it into my jeans pocket and tied the laces of my new shoes.

They were brown suede moccasins by a famous Italian brand, a generous present from Liliane for my first term as a student teacher.

My first term as a student teacher... If I said those words one more time, I'd have to swallow the entire pack of Immodim.

And today was only the first day back for the teachers.

I dreaded to think what state I'd be in when it came to facing my students.

Things had got off to a rough start. At the end of August, I had attended an induction session care of Creteil education authority that was worthy of sponsorship by Prozac. Neglect hung in the air. I soon realised the transition would come as a rude shock: we were being asked to go cold turkey as we made the radical switch from student to teacher.

As in all good detective stories, there was a good cop and a bad cop. Good cop opened the proceedings, sweating magnesium, vitamin C and enthusiasm from every pore. 'Many of you won't have chosen to be here,' he began cheerily. Next up was some baloney, in the vein of: *We need you!* This Uncle Sam, sent by the Department for Education, had a flair for faking joy. He was the kind of man who thinks all babies are beautiful. He also held that Creteil education authority was run with dynamism and passion. What can I say?

Bad cop, who kept his arms crossed throughout, stared at us for some time before glancing up at the strip-lighting and taking a deep breath.

'Being a teacher is a form of bereavement,' he declared, walking between the rows. 'That's right, bereavement. It means saying goodbye to your passion for literature, and mourning the loss of everything you've learned at university...'

As he glided between the chairs, he rattled off the list of

what we'd have to give up. Then came the reassuring bit: we'd be attending a training day, once a week, at the university institute for teacher training (IUFM) while, back in our host school, we'd be mentored by a teacher from the relevant department.

What can I say?

If we were being so well supported, why was the session entitled *How to give your first lesson* programmed for November? Just asking.

As I prepared for my 'bereavement' job, the days kept passing and there was still no information about the start of term, so I decided to phone my school-to-be.

My voice quavered when I asked to speak with the head, Monsieur Desclains, who, by contrast, sounded laid back.

'No cause for concern! It'll all be fine,' he kept saying.

At one point, he even laughed as if we were good friends. *Ho ho ho*, went his laugh. The laughter of men in positions of power is often *ho ho ho*. Take Father Christmas, for example, or the male bosses of top 40 companies listed on the French stock exchange, or any number of European heads of state.

The chattering classes, on the other hand, laugh with more of a *ha ha ha*, while marginalised communities go *he he he*.

He he he is definitely for minorities.

'Ho ho ho! Feeling anxious is perfectly normal! You'll enjoy yourself at our school, you'll see. The team at Gustave-Courbet is very friendly!'

When he said 'Gustave Courbet' I thought of that painting again, *The Origin of the World*. It was beginning to stress me out. What if I pictured it every time someone said 'Gustave Courbet'? Which, let's face it, was bound to happen a lot this year. As for the woman in the painting, I'd heard on the news that they'd located her face. Perhaps one day they'd locate her underwear too.

'I don't know what classes I've been assigned yet...'

'You'll have Year 7s and Year 9s, Monsieur Chennoun.'

'And what about the textbooks?'

'Well, normally speaking, we lend you those. You'll need to collect them from the library and learning resources centre.'

'Fine. When?'

'On the fourth of September.'

'So, that's on the first day of term, right?'

'Ho ho ho! Absolutely right. The first day of term.'

He didn't seem to think this was too late. Max relax.

In the end, I asked for details of the textbooks, which I bought in a bookshop, the Saint-Michel branch of Gibert Joseph.

Their titles? *The Eye and the Quill.* And the blockbusting, *Ink in Bloom.*

They must have found these in the Directory-of-Book-Titles-Rejected-at-the-Last-Minute.

Had that directory existed, its purpose would have been to index every author's ill-advised book title ideas. People could dip into it when stuck for a title for a text book, or on the hunt for an election campaign slogan.

Sitting in the métro with my journey planner, I worried about a violent onset of diarrohea the moment I had to introduce myself to my colleagues.

I must have re-read the summons for the teachers' INSET day 20 times. So I decided to take my mind off things by opening Dounia's book, making sure to keep it hidden behind my document wallet.

It started with a quote: *A touch of madness is almost always necessary for constructing a destiny.* Marguerite Yourcenar.

Under it, Dounia had written in my copy: 'I'd have liked for mine to have been constructed out of serenity. I've missed you.' On the next page, the book was dedicated to one Bernard T. T as in *Tantalising*. T as in *Tell us Who You Are*.

Chapter one began as follows: 'My father was a cobbler, but I haven't followed in his footsteps.'

I scanned the cover to check if Dounia hadn't co-written her book with a clown. No, she appeared to be the sole author responsible for this lame play on words. I tried reading a few lines as we trundled through two, then three, métro stations, but I was in no mood to concentrate. So I put the book away, while still worrying about my first day at work being ruined by acute diarrohea. I'd discovered that it was a genuine phobia. And a serious one at that. It even had a name: laxophobia.

I had finally reached the right place. After the métro, a bus ride. After the bus ride, a ten-minute walk.

There was a gigantic sign in front of the building, bearing the name of the collège (which I couldn't read because of the painting in my mind) and, hovering above the name, the logo for the departmental council of Seine-Saint-Denis. I buzzed at the gates which groaned on opening, like the review of a bad film.

Eight o'clock in the morning. Nobody around. *Looks like I'm the first person here,* I thought.

The main reception was deserted and I stared at the green lino, which was identical to the floor of the Neurovascular Unit at Nice University Hospital. It occurred to me that, right now, Big Baba would be eating his breakfast using his left hand; perhaps he'd spilled some coffee on its way to his mouth, or given up on buttering his toast.

I pictured him waking up, bleary-eyed, after nightmares filled with scary birdsong at dawn. Maybe it was just my nerves, but I felt a lump in my throat. Not that I cried, of course, because we all know that... Enough already.

Just then, in the distance, I spotted two strapping guys in tracksuits. One black, the other white. They were heading casually in my direction. The black guy whistled while the white one jangled his keyring. The sounds rang out in the empty reception area. They both had shaved heads, were tall and built like tanks. I remember thinking, *I bet they're the P.E. teachers.*

'Ha! On time?' the black guy got in first. 'So you're the new teacher, right?!'

I grinned idiotically and muttered a 'hello'.

'*Ho ho ho*! We spoke on the phone! You must be Monsieur Chennoun?' he said, with a firm handshake and a genuine smile. 'I'm Monsieur Desclains, the head.'

'Pleased to meet you', I replied.

Next, after stuffing his keyring into his tracksuit pocket, it was the white guy's turn to shake my hand: 'Hello! Monsieur Diaz, deputy head.'

'Nice to meet you. And I'm Monsieur Chennoun.'

'Welcome!'

'Thank you!'

In the middle of the reception area there was a table laid out with food: patisseries, orange juice and an enormous thermos of coffee.

'Go for it!' Diaz told me. 'Be our guest. Get stuck in!'

'Great!' I said, calculating that neither the coffee nor the orange juice would help my laxophobia.

The head and his deputy started joking about an ugly Spanish teacher with curves in all the right places.

'Her rear asset's worth a fortune,' Desclains joked to Diaz, as if I wasn't there, 'but her face is fit for bankruptcy.' They burst out laughing, Desclains's *ho ho ho* in harmony with Diaz's *ha ha ha*. Talk about misogynistic banter, I didn't know where to look.

My staffroom colleagues-to-be were arriving, one by one. They talked about their summer in Noirmoutier and compared notes on the progress of their offspring. I stood in one corner, chewing on a croissant, as overwhelmed as a timid son-in-law meeting his prospective family for the first time.

Three guys turned up together, looking like sales reps. Dark suits, pointy shoes and cheeks as smooth as the suave rally driver in that ad for electric razors. The oldest one had tightened his belt and hoisted his trousers well above his navel. A tribute to Jacques Chirac?

'Hey, here comes the sports crew!' someone called out.

If I'd got this right, the P.E. teachers were in suits and the head was in sportswear. Was I losing my grip? But the school term hadn't officially begun yet, and I sensed that everything would fall back into place tomorrow.

My soon-to-be colleagues stared at me from a distance. From time to time, a slim woman with brown hair flashed me a sympathetic smile. She was wearing a navy suit with ballerina pumps and her hair was pulled into a chignon. She reminded me of the Air France airhostess who gave me a colouring activity pack when we flew from Paris to Algiers in 1994. I had been enthralled by her beauty and kindness, to the point of confiding in Big Baba, 'I want to marry that lady!'

I remember it was only a few weeks before the hijacking of Air France flight 8969. My mother, who couldn't believe her eyes, was glued to the television right up until the moment when the plane was stormed by the National Gendarmerie Intervention Group (GIGN) in Marseille. As a small boy,

I was fascinated to watch the elite special forces, with their balaclavas and weapons, enter the plane. The list of hostages who had been killed was growing. The journalists were counting the number of gunshots fired. I kept thinking about my airhostess; about her smile, about how kind she'd been, and about my colouring activity pack.

On the news, we could see our Corsican interior minister, Charles Pasqua, commenting preacher-style on the armed intervention. Air France flights to Algeria were suspended after that.

'This time, it really is war,' Big Baba had proclaimed.

My cute colleague, who reminded me of the Air France airhostess, left her group to come and join me.

'Hi, I'm Hélène,' she said, holding out her hand. 'English teacher!'

It was funny, the way she introduced herself according to subject. She could as easily have said: 'Hi, I'm Hélène, European swimming champion.'

'Hi! And I'm Mourad, French teacher!'

'Aha!' she smiled. 'I knew it!

Turning to her group, she called out: 'You see! I was right! I win!'

She smiled at me again: 'It's just a little game we play, every time there's a new teacher.'

The *game* was to guess the subject taught by the fresh-off-the-boat kid.

'Don't stay on your own, come and join us!' urged the winner, patting me on the shoulder.

I glided after Hélène as if I were Mario, while other groups of teachers were clustering around the continental breakfast.

'*Hey hey*! She gives me moneeeey, when I'm in neeeed...' sang the English teacher in tribute to Ray Charles, as she held out her hand to her three colleagues. They each parted with €5, whether in note-form or as coins. After winding up her rendition of *I Got A Woman* and stuffing her winnings into her jacket pocket, Hélène introduced me to the rest of the team.

'So, this is Claude! History and Geography teacher! On his left, Caroline, Art teacher, and this is our friend Gérard, your fellow French teacher!'

'You'll see, it's friendly here,' said Caroline, who was small, blonde, barely older than me and wearing lots of colourful handmade jewellery. 'It's only my second year as well...' I stared at the two bright red lines emphasizing her lack of lips.

Gérard, in his fifties, cradled his bag as if it were a baby. I tried not to home in on his salt-and-pepper hair, because it made me faintly sick. That combo of natural graying mixed in with the original hair colour was the stuff of my worst nightmares, the colour of the obese old saddo.

'We'll see how long you last...' he said, looking me straight in the eye, no smile. Then he headed off to pour himself another cup of coffee.

The other three burst out laughing. He was clearly the group joker. The one who never missed a chance to make a snide remark as evidence of his brilliant mind.

Diaz clapped his hands four times to attract our attention.

'Dear friends, I'm going to ask you to follow me, please. We'll hold our meeting in the cafeteria.'

Instinctively, the teachers lined up in pairs. Professional conditioning. Next, we sat down at tables arranged in a U-shape, and Desclains handed everybody their personal timetable for the year.

'We've done our best to satisfy everybody!' he said, cocking an eyebrow.

I scanned mine. I would be working Tuesday to Friday.

Mondays, my day of respite, would be reserved for my teacher training days.

'Oh my! They're not giving you an easy ride this year...' Hélène whispered over my shoulder.

Next, Diaz passed each of us a small file containing headshots of the students in our classes. The teachers were like over-excited teenagers experiencing sudden hormone releases.

'Fuck me!' someone exclaimed, staring at the mugshots in front of him. 'This can't be true? What've I done to deserve this? Another year with Mehdi Mazouani?' He pointed to one student's photo. 'D'you really want my suicide on your conscience?'

A few chuckles.

I checked the photos and names in front of me and noticed that Mehdi Mazouani, the boy apparently capable of driving a man to suicide, also appeared on my Year 9 class list.

The more I scrutinised the faces of the students I was about to teach, the more I realised how unattractive teenagers can look. Greasy skin, dubious hairstyles, vacant eyes. That's how I looked at 14.

When it came to my turn to introduce myself, I didn't suffer from instant and debilitating diarrohea. I listened to my fellow teachers. They talked about breaktime, about supervising this or that strategic area, about when the school nurse was on duty and about everybody contributing to the cost of the Senseo coffee pods for the staffroom coffee machine.

None of this was my problem yet. I just inhaled the waves of vanilla perfume wafting over from Hélène, as I reflected on how much I liked her name. It reminded me of that song by George Brassens, *Les Sabots d'Hélène.*

New Face

Liliane's apartment was rammed like a Line 6 carriage at 6.40pm, in the evening rush-hour. Now that I'm more familiar with Paris, I'm sneaking the City of Light into my similes. All Miloud's friends had headed over, from *Le Saphir Bleu* as well as further afield. Mario had even broken sweat. *Visible proof that he's human, after all!* I thought to myself.

A lavish spread had been laid on for the occasion, with Miloud hiring the caterer Liliane used for important dinners. Guests were being served canapés by the waiters. Miloud's friend Sousou, who worked in the cloakroom at *Le Saphir Bleu*, was savouring the food with her eyes closed. 'Mmmmmm!' she gushed, chewing on a mouthful of prawn as knowingly as any self-respecting foodie. 'This is delicious! It melts in the mouth. It's tender and salty, it's spicy and suggestive, I mean we're talking off the scale here, you get me...?'

Miloud roared with laughter. 'Haaa! *Soukti*! Shut up and eat! D'you think you're on *Masterchef*?'

Sousou shrugged, as if to say, 'You've got no idea!' Then she snapped her fingers at one of the waiters. 'Hey, you, Baby Cakes, c'me here!' And, straight up, she demanded the recipe for the prawn canapés. The waiter's eyes bulged.

Another faux pas: asking for the caterer's secret recipes.

'What? Don't you understand my question? Am I speaking Chinese or something?'

'I'll find out for you, Madame...' replied the fresh-faced waiter, looking disconcerted.

Meanwhile, a man was stubbing out his cigarette on a sculpture by Liliane's favourite Danish artist. *Shitty ashtray* he must have thought, crushing his cigarette butt against the small statuette.

Another man was staring at a modernist painting, tilting his head to the right, then to the left.

'Is it upside down?' he asked, turning to me for help.

I glanced at it.

'No.'

'*Tfi'ch*', snorted the guy, doing something curious with his lower lip. Tfi'ch is Arabic for 'load of old rubbish'.

To be honest, on closer inspection he wasn't wrong. I'd even go so far as to say *Tfi'ch* would make the perfect title for that painting.

Naturally, there was raï playing everywhere. A party organised by Miloud without raï would be like an African country that has rich mineral reserves and is at peace.

A woman with an enormous backside climbed onto the magnificent black piano in the middle of the room, transforming it into a vulgar night club podium. I could see her stilettos scratching the surface and it made me feel queasy.

'Oi! You up there!' Miloud called out, reacting at last. He was staring at the woman, who paused to look down at him from her platform.

'Make some space for me!' he added with a wink.

Miloud clambered up and grabbed the woman by the waist. 'Ahmed! Ahmed! Play Cheb Houcem again!' he shouted in the direction of one of his friends. Most of the guests began chanting: 'Cheb Houcem! Cheb Houcem!'

According to Miloud, one of the Cheb's songs had become

the second Algerian national anthem. My cousin always has to talk things up.

Liliane was staying in the clinic for a few days because of her facelift. Soon, there would be the unveiling of her new face.

Miloud had the apartment to himself... not counting Mario, or the two cleaners working alternate shifts. He was as excited as a teenager planning a secret party with his parents away.

Before the chauffeur drove his boss to the beauty clinic, I'd been treated to the heart-rending farewell scene.

Miloud and Liliane had insisted on saying their goodbyes as if it were forever. As if they might never see each other again. She clung to him. He ruffled her hair and kissed her head, forehead and neck, over and over again, like some kind of pagan ritual.

'Oh my Miloud!' she sighed

'I love you, my true love!' Miloud ventured, with tears in his eyes. 'You make me so happy, you're the woman of my dreams!' He was pulling out all the stops. If she hadn't been post-menopausal, he'd probably have added, 'And I want you to be the mother of my children.'

Liliane was frightened of going under the surgeon's knife. The first time, when she was 13 and on holiday at the house of her great-uncle (who happened to own the finest vineyards in Champagne) she had undergone an emergency operation for acute peritonitis. That was when she discovered a fear of dying, which would never leave her.

The second time was for the birth of Edouard. A caesarian with complications. She said the scar was still painful sometimes, like a son's absence.

Liliane's remark turned my thoughts towards my own mother. Deep down, mothers are all the same, or nearly.

They suffer. They love with their guts. 'El kebda, el kebda.' Liliane also had organs that oozed maternal affection. The difference was that she didn't wring out her bleeding liver in front of her son at the first opportunity. Then again, my mother didn't frequent sleazy clubs on the arms of a blédard almost 30 years her junior. She didn't plan on getting her cheeks scalped either.

My mother's cheeks are soft and still plump. Her wrinkles are the lines of the book she's never been able to write. Her life story is drawn in the corners of her eyes. The creases on her brow trace all the worries, the times waiting up after dark and the health scares.

A mother is like a great destiny: beautiful and harsh at the same time.

Rue Michel-Ange, the party was in full swing and everybody seemed to be enjoying themselves. That said, this crowd would have enjoyed itself wherever it was.

A young man who couldn't stop laughing was sprawled on Liliane's armchair, sucking on a shisha pipe. He was trying to blow various smoke rings, reminding me of the Caterpillar in *Alice in Wonderland*.

'Want some? It's green olive and candied lemon flavour!' he laughed, holding out his shisha in slow motion.

'No thanks, I'm fine.'

That didn't stop him laughing. *Huh huh huh* went his laugh. *Huh huh huh* is the laugh of an observer. Journalists, shrinks and sport commentators go *huh huh huh*.

'What's so funny?'

'Take a good look at them. What I've noticed is the less secure their legal status, the more they throw themselves about. The undocumented ones are wild: they knock back the drink, dancing and laughing with their mouths wide open.

Those on student visas and short-term visas are more laid back, they laugh quietly. But check the most relaxed of all: the ones with ten-year residence permits. Watch 'em! Ten years! Chill! They smoke, they sit comfortably, they think they can reshape the world because they belong to it.'

'What about me?'

He burst out laughing again.

'*Huh huh huh*! You're going round and round in circles. You switch rooms. You leave, you come back. You're trying to find where you fit in and it's no fun. I reckon you were born here.'

The Freud of the party.

To prove him wrong, I decided to dance. To relax and let go. To throw myself around with wild abandon like someone undocumented.

I'd only just started trying out my moves when a girl stared at me and sniggered. She was petite and blonde with several centimetres of black roots.

'Boiii!' she said. 'You're like a sick goat!'

Luckily, I'm not the touchy type. I carried on dancing and laughing away, pretending I hadn't heard. She came and put her hands on my waist to show me what I was meant to do. Those warm hands made me blush. I think she found my shyness amusing.

'What's up with your hips? Have they got a sick note from the doctor, or what? Come on, move! Listen to the music!'

No matter how much I tried listening, I couldn't catch the rhythm.

'I don't believe it, you keep missing the beat! It's not like it's difficult. In the rain, you'd be the only one to stay dry! You'd be passing between the raindrops! I've never seen anything like it!'

She turned her back on me with a scornful shrug of her shoulders.

I gave up dancing. For good.

The woman with the enormous backside was still perched on the piano-podium. She held her silver clutch bag to her chest while raising the other arm to the ceiling, glass in hand. A Statue of Liberty who'd overdone it with hot dogs.

I caught up with Miloud in heated discussion with his pals. One of them was giving him a hard time. My cousin kept staring uncomfortably at his feet, without saying anything. Every so often he would shake his head.

'You think she'll agree to marry you, this old Froggie of yours? That she'll get your papers sorted for you? Dream on, Miloud! You're a thing, to her, an object. Like her vases or her armchair, or that ugly picture hanging on the wall. When she's had enough of you, she'll kick you out and find herself a new toy. What are you going to do if something happens to your parents, eh? They're old! Your mother's diabetic! D'you realise she has to have insulin injections every day? Have you sent her any money instead of blowing everything the old hag gives you on clothes and cars? Your family's counting on you! D'you realise that?'

Miloud lowered his head again. Any further and he'd break his neck.

'Wakey-wakey! It's shameful! Everyone here's thinking the same thing. But no one dares tell you!'

Miloud couldn't take any more of Moral Highground guilt-tripping him.

'You'd have done the same in my shoes!'

'Never!' protested Moral Highground. 'By everything I cherish! Never! May Allah be my witness! I hold to my values and my upbringing! Where's your nif? Eh? Call yourself Algerian? The pride of a true Algerian has no price! You traded yours for a set of new teeth and a Mercedes! H'chouma, Miloud!'

Miloud was offended, big time.

'Stop! Calm down!' the other guys kept telling them.

Moral Highground put on his coat, his mutterings drowned out by the music. I figured he was Sousou's boyfriend from the way he jerked his head in her direction, indicating 'Yallah, let's go!' This didn't stop her from insisting the fresh-faced waiter wrap a few servings of prawn in foil as a takeaway.

The next day, poor Mario, the perennial pre-dawn riser, had cleaned the apartment from top to bottom as well as preparing a hearty breakfast. Not a hint of tiredness on his deadpan face. Even the heel marks on the piano, left by the woman with the enormous backside, had vanished. The man was a magician.

As for Miloud, he was poleaxed by a strong migraine and couldn't get out of bed. He'd fallen asleep in his jeans, with his shirt half-unbuttoned.

'An aspirin, cuz, I'm begging you!' he pleaded through half-closed eyes, when I popped my head round the door. His tongue was furred and white and he struggled to finish the soluble tablet I gave him.

'Too many worries inside here,' Miloud explained, putting the glass on the bedside table and pointing to his head. I nodded and tried to look sympathetic.

'I'm going to call my mum today,' he added in a last-ditch effort.

At breakfast, Mario brought me the day's papers. On the back cover of a major daily, Dounia's smouldering eyes, her chin in the palm of her left hand, and that gaze which seemed to say, 'You can't imagine how intelligent I am.'

The title of the interview was *The New Face of Feminism.* The journalist, one Anne-Marie Sistitis, asked Dounia about her 'authoritarian, change-averse, illiterate father' and about her mother who 'reproduced, in spite of herself, an upbringing aimed at destroying any sort of self-realisation, encarcerating her emotions inside the rich sauces of the dishes she cooked, inside the cakes she baked, forcing Dounia to eat every last morsel at mealtimes'.

And so I was led to understand that my mother would have forced Dounia to grow fat, with the sole aim of destroying her daughter's body image and distancing her forever from her own desires as a woman. A diabolical plan shrewdly executed.

I wondered if there was anything in the penal code about 'premeditated force-feeding'.

Perhaps one day we would see this journalist, with that infected name of hers that cried out for a dose of antibiotics, interviewing my mother, who would in turn have written her own book, entitled: *Fed Up Of Being Sexually Objectified? Try Morbid Obesity!*

Following its stratospheric success, of the kind not seen since *Men Are From Mars, Women Are From Venus*, she would be urged to follow-up with volume two: *Made To Feel Like A Piece Of Meat? Eat More Beef!*

I was sad to read so many humiliating remarks about my family. Dounia wasn't faring any better than the faceless woman in Courbet's painting, I figured. At least the artist's muse ended up finding her own face, even if it did take centuries.

In this 'heartfelt' interview, Dounia expained that she had gone into politics to change things, and that in order to succeed she needed to operate from inside the system.

'You don't need to taste the pepper to discover it's hot,' Big Baba often used to say. 'Just sniff it and your eyes will weep already.'

I resolved to dip back into my sister's book, *The Price of Freedom*. By my reckoning, the price she had paid was exorbitant. Plus, she hadn't specified that this was a group tariff. We were all paying for her shitty freedom, and we'd been doing so for years.

An article like that in a national newspaper was going to be difficult to ignore. I suspected that plate tectonics would trigger reactions as far away as Nice and beyond.

It was Sunday morning and I bit down hard on one of those succulent rhubarb brioches, which might one day become my Proustian madeleine.

The Tank

First floor. Room 107. A line of disorderly teenagers. My Year 7s, shoulders hunched under the weight of their schoolbags, had formed small army oiled with sebum ready to do battle with me. There they stood, grown-ups in-the-making – I could picture them, in ten or 15 years' time, their shoulders even more stooped under the weight of worries.

I had already spotted two or three of them in the playground, watching me as I parked the car. Now, seeing the same kids whispering as I made my approach, I realised it was a bad idea to bring the Mercedes. It was Miloud who had insisted I borrow it.

Mourad, chill out, be zen, I told myself, trying to get a firm grip on my classroom keys. But they began dancing in my clammy hand, threatening to slip away at any second.

'Good morning!' I said opening the door and avoiding eye contact.

'Morning, sir,' a few replied.

Immodium. Immodium. Immodium. Immodium.

I pushed open the door, trying not to think about my laxophobia, and stared coldly at my students.

'Come in!' I said.

They filed calmly into the classroom, one behind another, in such orderly fashion it felt like I had won the lottery.

'Sit down!' I ordered, trying out the next intruction.

No sooner said than done. *Holy shit,* I recall thinking, *they follow orders!* This was deeply satisfying, but it was also as if I were watching myself in action. For someone who was meant to embody authority, I sensed I was an impostor.

I wrote my name on the board, making sure to curl the C of Chennoun nicely. I began by writing my name because, in all my classroom memories, the teachers began by writing their name in big letters on the blackboard. They stamped us with it for life, like livestock: *Remember this name.*

I asked my students to do the same thing on half sheets of paper. Some of the girls wrote in pink, and drew hearts where the dots should have been on their i's, or added little flowers around their first names. Others, at the back, wrote in insect-sized handwriting and I couldn't begin to make it out.

A girl in the front row was slouched at her desk, playing with her cornrows, as I tried to decipher her half-page.

'Cassandra!' I said in my newly-appointed-boss voice, "Sit up, please!"

It worked a treat, because Cassandra sat up straight for the rest of the lesson and, for all I know, will continue to do so for the rest of her life. 'Have you noticed?' she'll ask her osteopath, when she's 30. 'My spine is flawless! It's all thanks to my French teacher, who said to me one day...'

In that moment, I felt I could expect anything of them: rigour... excellence... the moon.

But I didn't have a clue, so what I asked them was: "Right, what do you think we're going to do this year?'

'Reading and writing...! Spelling...! Grammar...!' came a few answers fired from different parts of the classroom.

I responded by scribing their replies, to enjoy the feeling of chalk gliding across the board, '*Reading and writing!* Yes!

Spelling! Very good! And *Grammar!* Yes!'

This meant that the first interruption caught me off-guard, and with my back turned.

I could hear one of my female students acting the troublemaker. Or perhaps it was one of my male students; they can be hard to distinguish at that age.

The voice struck me in the back: shrill, sharp as an arrow and singing, '*Shine bright liiiike a diamond*!'

Laughter all round to the effect that this was the joke of the century. As well as being ugly, teenagers have a sense of humour that sucks.

For a split second I wondered what to do. This was their way of testing me. The famous test. How could I ever have thought I'd dodge it? I carried on staring at the board, playing the person who wouldn't be knocked off balance, not even by an earthquake measuring eight on the Richter scale.

'Grammar might come in handy for you too, Rihanna!' I ventured.

It started up again, scattered laughter around the room, clinging to everything: walls, ceiling, blackboard. Acne-pocked belly laughs.

'Right, that's enough!' I said. Then I cleared my throat and tried again, even louder: 'That's enough!'

But they didn't stop.

That's when I realised dangling a carrot wasn't going to work. And humour wasn't the solution either. This was all-out war and my job was to become an armoured vehicle, a tank on auto-pilot. I didn't have a choice, it was *imperative*. If tanks alone survive in war zones, it's because they're solid and they're bombproof.

After a brief lull, I asked my students to fill out their 'About Me' sheets, which would provide a little more information:

parental occupations, siblings, hobbies.

I thought fondly back to Madame Mocca, my History and Geography teacher, who was close to retirement age when I started at secondary school. She was the proprietor of the establishment. You could tell from the way she had personalised her classroom. There were green plants dotted about and she had pinned photos of her grandchildren to the wall, as well as the inevitable relief maps of France.

We were chez-Madame Mocca, and, chez-Madame Mocca, she was the law. She was old and so slight that we were scared she might break a bone with each step she took. But it was a false impression of frailty. You could hear a pin drop in her lessons. Everything ran like clockwork. Madame Mocca was a rare kind of tank, embodying natural authority in all its splendour.

At parents' evening, she had remarked to Big Baba, who was wearing his suit with the Bic biros clipped to his jacket pocket: 'If I only had Mourads in my class, everything would be perfect.'

Big Baba had grinned from ear to ear. We could see all his fillings as a token of how proud he was.

'Sir? If our parents aint working, isn't it we put benefits?' asked a student at the back, who hadn't bothered to take off her coat before raising her hand.

I collected the 'About Me' sheets slowly, stringing things out, like an Italian football team leading in extra time.

Another student, who was leaning on the radiator, asked permission to speak.

'Sir? Is it true you sell weed?'

'I beg your pardon?!'

'Word is, you're dealin' – that's what a Year 9 told us this morning.'

Dozens of pairs of eyes were staring at me now, hanging on my answer as if I were about to utter words of prophesy.

'So what kind of rumour is this?'

'He said there's a teacher, yeah, and we all know teachers aint zillionaires, but this one, he said, he's driving a C-class Merc.'

'So, in your view, if a teacher drives a nice car it automatically means they're selling drugs?'

'Nah, but you're Arab innit?'

Bad idea, borrowing Miloud's car. Very bad idea.

'Would anyone like to tell us what a cliché is?'

The responses came quick as a flash:

'A cliché? Isn't that like a photo?'

'Cliché-sous-Bois? That's where my aunt lives!'

So I spent my first lesson explaining that clichés often reflect prejudices or snap judgements.

'Is it like when people say gingers smell?' asked Sylvestre, a short redhead in the front row.

'Absolutely, Sylvestre!'

'But that's not a cliché, sir,' piped up a voice from the southern border of the classroom, 'it's the truth. Carrot tops do smell – of wee!'

Everyone burst out laughing again.

'Shhhhhhh!' I hushed them, remembering my colleague Gérard, whose classroom was next door.

The bell rang. Everyone stood up at once. Proper little soldiers. Out they trooped, in tight formation. One, two, one, two, march. A few checked their mobiles, which wrong-footed me. A smartphone in Year 7? I'd never felt so prehistoric.

Next up was what teachers call a 'window'. A free hour between two lessons. Time to revive my spirits.

A student returned shyly to the classroom.

'Sorry, sir. I left my Ventolin on the table, and if I have an asthma attack I might die, that's what my mum said.'

'Right, come on in, then.'

Dodging between the desks, she picked up her inhaler and stuffed it into a pocket.

'Sir, is this your first time as a teacher ?

'What did you say your name was?'

'Asma Zerdad. But everyone teases me about it.'

'Why? Asma's a pretty name.'

'They still tease me, though. It's because I'm asthmatic.'

'I see.'

'But I don't care. They're stupid. Is this your first time, sir, because the new teachers, well, none of them stay. I mean, they always leave at the end of the year. Or that's what my big sister says.'

'Is she a student here, your sister?'

'Yeah, she's in Year 9. She's called Sarah.'

'Well, here's hoping everything goes to plan and I can stay.'

'Insha'Allah, sir. Good luck. I'd better go, I'll be late.'

Her schoolbag was so wide she could barely squeeze through the door, and then Asma was gone. A little girl whose mother probably still brushed her hair (the brightly coloured scrunchies in the long plait she wore to one side were a giveaway). She reminded me of my sister Mina, when she was younger.

Prior to my first day, I'd been worrying about the verdict of the inspector who, at the end of my teacher-training year, would randomly decide whether I deserved to qualify or not.

Now, my only question was whether or not I'd make it through 'til the end of the school year.

Following a succession of Year 7s, all exhibiting varying degrees of restlessness or enthusiasm, the morning was finally over.

I began to create a character for myself: Vladimir, a man with no pity or remorse, raised in the tundra by a pack of wolves.

The teachers had their own area in the cafeteria. A sort of bunker, arrived by braving hordes of starving teenagers and crossing a fanfare of clinking knives and forks.

All those emotions had made me hungry, and I piled my tray with a meal fit for a pregnant woman at full term. Potato, I insisted on plenty of potato, I wanted heaps of the stuff. I had a plate filled with enough starch to last me through war.

I headed for Hélène, seeking out her vanilla scent and compassionate smile as my antidote. The seat next to her was taken by Gérard. Elbows bolted to the table, he was chewing on his spaghetti bolognaise and smearing it all over his moustache.

He shot me one of his sardonic looks.

'Still alive?'

'Yes, as you can see.'

'They were running riot with you, hey? You do realise I'm in the next door classroom and I can hear everything?'

Yes, you blockhead with the disgusting salt-and-pepper hair, I do realise! was the answer I wanted to give.

'Sure, they're upbeat students. I like it that way, it keeps things lively!'

'Lively? Ha-ha!'

He carried on slurping his spaghetti.

Gérard was assuming the role of the threatened elder, keen to outsmart me. Let him mock me all he liked, he had yet to meet Vladimir, my steely double, who would have opted for raw bear meat at the cafeteria.

Hélène smiled and raised a cherry tomato to her mouth, pointing to the empty chair opposite Gérard. 'Have a seat there, Mourad!'

She looks nice with her hair down, I thought as I slid my tray onto the table.

There was also a new face, a young guy in his thirties with an unruly lock of hair that he kept blowing out of the way. This was something I could only do in my dreams, but, given the texture of my hair, I'd shaved off those dreams with a pair of clippers.

'Hi, I'm Wilfried,' he said, holding out his hand. 'I'm the long-term supply teacher.'

'Pleased to meet you, Wilfried.'

'First day not proving too painful?'

'Could be worse,' I ventured, remembering the expression 'glass half-full'.

'So what does long-term supply teaching involve?'

Wilfried smiled and performed that trick again with his slick lock of hair.

'It's means I'm of no-fixed-abode in the education system. I've been here for a year and a half now, filling in for the librarian. It's the first time I've stayed so long in one place.'

'What happened to the librarian?' I asked, shovelling down the potatoes.

Hélène and Gérard exchanged a knowing look.

Wilfried smirked and cut up his steak carefully.

'You're sure you want to know?'

'Why? Am I not meant to?'

'She got it in the face with a fire extinguisher – big gash above the eyes. You can still see the bloodstain on the learning resources centre carpet. Nothing life-threatening, but she's been deeply traumatised.'

'You don't say... ?!'

'Extended sick leave...you see where I'm coming from...'

'Stop it! You'll frighten him!' Hélène remonstrated. I love dusting down the verb 'to remonstrate'. Not that I often get the chance.

'Don't worry about me, I'm fine.'

'Trouble is, she really *was* a piece of work...!'

'Nobody deserves to be hit with a fire extinguisher,' added Gérard, with a spurt of tomato sauce. 'Nobody.'

'Sure, but she pushed her luck.... Anyway, it's not like Wilfried has any worries in that department, all the girls are head-over-heels in love with him. He's a catch!'

'You're exaggerating, Hélène!'

'No I'm not! They're all crazy for you!'

'Rubbish! *He he he.* Stop it, you'll make me blush! Right, I'm off to find some dessert!'

Wilfried covered his embarrassment by standing up and loping aimably towards the dessert section.

'What those girls don't realise,' added Gérard, unable to resist as he mopped up the remains of his sauce with some bread, 'is that, however crazy they are for him, he'll always be the 'craziest girl' of all!'

He guffawed and his moustache quivered like a row of sardines.

Hélène's disapproving expression made her look extra cute.

'Keep your homophobic jokes to yourself, Gérard.'

I reckon I'd have figured out sooner or later that the L-T-S teacher was a bit G-A-Y.

'So tell me, new-kid-on-the-block,' said Gérard, standing up, 'what's your union status?'

'Because,' said Hélène, raising one eyebrow irresistibly,

'Gérard is the union rep around here...'

'So if you decide to join up, kiddo, come and see me. We're CGT at Gustave Courbert.'

Would that be CGT, as in the General Workers' Union? Or CGT as in *Cretin with Grey Tufts*?

Gérard the salt-and-pepper union rep, with his bolognese-spattered moustache, suddenly started talking more softly.

'You haven't given me an answer about Thursday evening, Hélène...'

'Thursday evening? What's happening on Thursday evening?'

'Hey, come on, it's the preview of my friend's photography exhibition, remember, at the mairie de Montreuil...'

'Oh yeah, of course... Look, I don't know yet, Gérard, I'll keep you posted. I've got no idea what I'm doing on Thursday evening, it's a long way off...'

'A long way off? It's in three days' time...'

'I'll let you know, okay?'

The union rep recused himself, wiping his moustache with the back of his hand. Thwarted and revolting.

'Between you and me, Mourad, Gérard's a bit heavy-going. He doesn't mean any harm, but he's heavy-duty.'

You don't say? I didn't say.

Gérard had lost his first match. I experienced a rush of pleasure, heightened by the warm spuds I was wolfing down.

Wilfried, the long-term supply teacher, was on his way back to our table when he noticed our salt-and-pepper rep stomping out of the canteen.

'So what's up with Gérard? Why's he in a huff?'

At least Wilfried could distinguish between 'normal' Gérard and Gérard 'in a huff'.

Because I couldn't see any difference.

The Big Bare Truth

I was the one who suggested Miloud buy flowers, because I thought Liliane would appreciate the gesture.

'But I don't know the first thing about flowers!' Miloud admitted.

In the end, we opted for an arrangement at €39.90. Top of the range.

'So much dough for something that'll fade tomorrow! Tfi'ch!'

Now Miloud was playing at being thrifty.

Liliane's face was still in bandages.

'Oooohhhhnooooomiiiiihouuuuuuuuyooooooooo-caaaaaaaaaseeeeeeemeeeeeeeeeliiiiiiiithhhaaaaaa!' she said, when we turned up in her room. She waved her arms in slow motion, like a tortoise on its back, and hid her face.

If I listened carefully, I thought I could just make out the words: *Oh no! My Miloud ! You can't see me like this*!

'You look like an Egyptian mummy!' Miloud burst out laughing.

There was a knock at the bedroom door.

'Cooooooo-iiiiiii,' said Liliane.

Stone the crows! I thought, as soon as the doctor entered. *What an enormous head!*

As well as being endowed with a broad forehead, the back

of this man's skull was super bulbous. As in, fresh brains coming to the boil and about to spill over.

When I was a boy, I used to think the size of your head was in direct proportion to how clever you were. I often heard people say of me: 'He's got a head on him!' And I would picture how, factoring in time and books and all those years of study, my cranium would swell up like a balloon on the verge of exploding.

'Hello! I'm Doctor El Koubi!' said the man, shaking us by the hand and proceeding to make a few unfunny jokes. Medical humour. His geometric smile, which was almost triangular, could have modelled an explanation of Pythagorus' theorem. It made him look untrustworthy. Like a liar.

Doctor El Koubi told us how Liliane's procedure had gone, tossing words like *elasticitity, epidermis* and *muscle tone* into the air, before juggling them, but he soon realised we weren't interested. I kept thinking back to that video, the one featuring a mad meat-carver of a Spanish surgeon with Stevie Wonder playing in the background.

'Good, right, well, I think the time has come to remove your bandages, all right... good... all right...'

He punctuated everything with *good, all right, good, all right...* together with his isoceles triangle smile. Liliane waved her hands in the air and kept on muttering into her bandages, tilting her head to one side: 'Haaaheeeheeennnnnndeeehhhaaaaahheeemeeeennnn!'

Full disclosure, this time I struggled to translate her.

'Now, the appearance may be rather shocking at first,' said Doctor El Koubi, erring on the side of caution as he snipped delicately at Liliane's bandages. 'You'll recall that we had a little chat about this...? It will all change, of course, but it's always a bit swollen to begin with, and there's likely to be some bruising ...'

Given all the warnings, we were expecting to see the Elephant Man.

What appeared was Liliane's face: the same, but stretched tight, and covered in bruises.

I asked Doctor El Koubi Mega-Head if people ever reclaimed their removed skin. After all, those pieces belonged to them. The skin from your face, belly and bum is personal, right? If I'd been a surgeon, I'd have deemed a request like that perfectly reasonable. What people did with those pieces of skin was their own business, even if it involved sprinkling them into their chorba.

El Koubi gave me a peculiar look and shook his head. As if I'd just weirded him out with my question. As if it was weirder than spending your days breaking noses, sucking fat off hips and stuffing rubber inserts into boobs.

I asked him because my mother had been adamant about keeping my foreskin.

I was four or five. Which is too old to be circumcised, by the way. It's not right to be able to recall a moment like that. It was the start of the Nineties. The month of August in the swelter of Algiers. There was a small crowd thronging around me. I was wearing a strange outfit and my mother kept bursting into tears every time I caught her eye.

Our neighbour, Hadhoum the tobacco chewer, had kissed me on both cheeks and slid a blue note into my tunic, which Big Baba didn't waste any time in collecting.

'Give that to me, my son,' he whispered, 'I'll go and buy you some ice-cream...'

As the women prepared the meal, the pressure cooker hissed in the kitchen.

'What are they doing?' asked my grandmother. 'It's nearly

time for noon prayers! They'll be late for Dhuhr!'

And then she frowned, the way she always did when she was vexed, distorting the green tatoo on her face.

'The sheikh's coming for several boys in the neighbourhood,' said Hind, one of my aunts, whose cheeks were streaming with tears because of the onions she was chopping. 'He's doing them all on the same day, it takes time...'

It was foreskin carnage in Algiers that day.

The old sheikh, clad in white, was patrolling the streets of Bab el Oued, armed with his pair of scissors to settle scores with all the little boys' willies in the Algerian capital.

Dounia came out onto the balcony to find me.

'They're going to cut if off. They're going to cut it off!' she declared, creased up with laughter.

I had no idea what she was talking about, but she seemed thrilled.

'Will he feel any pain?' asked Mina, anxiously. 'Will he bleed a lot?'

Cut it off? Bleed a lot?

That was when I started having flashbacks to Eid el-Kebir. *Now I get it,* I thought, *they're going to slit my throat!*

I had already been experiencing night terrors, given all my grandmother's tales about the men from the east of the country slitting the throats of village babies, and my mother had been having a dreadful time calming me down afterwards....

My turn has come, I thought. *Maybe there's a shortage of sheep in the region, so they've dressed me in white to make me look like a lamb, and one of my uncles, the one who never smiles, will sharpen his big knife against the stone stairs, and then, schlack!, he'll slit my throat just like that!*

Shortly afterwards, we heard the women making their

youyous. Then the men pinned me down by the arms and legs. I put up a bit of struggle, although not much of one, looking back on it.

The sheikh with his small round glasses had smiled as he stroked my head, temporily reassuring me. Next, he took out his shiny scissors and cleaned them. *Why are they doing this to me?* I remember thinking. *I haven't done anything wrong today! I didn't even wet my bed! It's not fair!*

When I felt the sheikh's dry hands, it all became clear. I started crying and looking to Big Baba for support, but he did nothing to help.

'Don't cry, don't cry...' was all he could say. Same as always.

If you'd given me the choice there and then, I'd have opted to have my throat slit. Now that I'm an adult, and with the benefit of hindsight, I'm glad to have got rid of that thing.

My mother was making eyes at my father from a distance and miming the action she required of him: 'Pick up the foreskin! Pick it up, Abdelkader!'

My father rolled his eyes at what he deemed an idiotic request, but he still bent down with a sigh to pick up my foreskin from the rug and carry it over to my mother.

'This is insane! You need treatment!'

Maman placed this peculiar trophy in a paper handkerchief.

I was given special treatment for several days. I had been brave and it was as if I finally deserved respect.

I regaled Ismaël, my younger cousin, with my epic story. I could read the fear in his eyes, and it made me feel strong and important.

A beautiful winter light filled the room in the clinic. We could now see the whole truth of Liliane's face.

Miloud managed to hold back his laughter, but he couldn't stop himself from whispering in my ear, 'She looks like a white Mike Tyson!'

Liliane seemed dissatisfied, and not even the triangular smiles of Doctor El Koubi, hovering behind her like a small demon in the mirror, could convince her that the operation had been a success.

I had forgotten to bring my mobile with me. Not that anyone ever rang it.

Once we were back at Liliane's apartment, I was stopped in my tracks by the display of '17 Missed Calls'. I felt as if the Red Army Choir were inside my chest.

My voicemail chopped up every syllable in its distinctive voice, while declaring: *Un-worth-y son, you're in for a do-zen mes-sag-es from your hys-ter-i-cal mo-ther, good luck!*

'You've seen it? You've seen it, the newspaper?' began the first message. 'Mina read the whole thing out loud to me! Yééé! Ya Rabi! H'choumaaaaaa! Dig my grave now! Bury me alive! In a hole, somewhere in the garden!! Hide my face! Cover me with earth! I'm already covered with shame!'

A voicemail-Greek-tragedy mash-up. All that was missing was: 'Call me back, lots of love – it's Phaedra, by the way.'

'So I've suffered all my life to endure this?' went Maman's second message. 'Why did I come to this ungrateful country? Why did I follow a countryman from the West I didn't even know? Do you realise how beautiful I was as a young woman? I could have married the Algerian Minister for Gas and Petroleum! I could have married a prince! Instead of which, I married a cobbler! A cobbler who nailed me to France! He nailed me here, just like he nailed his shoes! And now I've been humiliated by the monster I gave birth to! She talks about marriage! We didn't force her to do anything! He was a boy from a good family! She agreed, and then she changed her mind from one day to the next! No one held a knife to her throat! And the photo! Have you seen it?! She's cut her hair! She looks like a boy! Tffffou!'

I'll spare you the third, fourth and fifth messages, which were variations on a theme.

The sixth doesn't count (two minutes twenty-eight of sobbing).

The seventh and eighth were overly violent and not adapted for modern civilisation.

The ninth message got my undivided attention:

'It's my fault. I've ruined everything. I didn't want my children to be good people, I wanted my children to be perfect! I expected too much of them! Too much!'

Self-doubt. For the first time! If I'd been my mother, I'd have said 'H'marmette'. Given the singular rarity of this event, her message didn't just mark one donkey dying, but the entire species disappearing for good.

To-save-press-one instructed the mocking voicemail, and of course I pressed one (unlike the other messages which I deleted by pressing two).

To start your life ov-er and be-gin ag-ain from ze-ro, press four, is what I'd like to have heard the cold automated voice saying. Like a fool, I'd have pressed four, only to hear the same voice laughing: *Huh huh huh, id-i-ot, no-bo-dy can e-ver be-gin ag-ain from ze-ro, not ev-en the A-ra-bs who in-ven-te-d it, as your Big Ba-ba would say…*

My mother had said 'too much, too much' as if she were suffocating.

Too much suffering? Too much love? Too many rules?

Not that I'm convinced too many rules leads to breaking them. If they're fair, there could be a heap of rules for everything under the sun and it wouldn't bother anyone.

It's the excess of love I find frightening.

'El kebda, el kebda.' This display of guts and intestines is damaging. It comes with impossible demands and culminates in a despotic regime. The upshot? A woman in her thirties with sorrowful eyes, reduced to skin and bones. And there's the heart of the matter: a lack of flesh arising from a lack of love. A woman who feels unrecognised and forsaken, making front page headlines to tell the whole world what she couldn't say to her own mother and father, despite their love and good intentions.

But good intentions aren't always enough. Some things need saying.

I don't know why, but I thought of little Asma in my Year 7 class, with her multi-coloured scunchies. Did she too have a mother so crushing she had developed asthma?

Mario interrupted me while my ear was still glued to my mobile. I had my back to him and he couldn't see that I was otherwise engaged, or he would never have disturbed me. He was too qualified for that, too squeaky clean. Someone had disinfected him at birth. He'd been bottlefed bleach as a baby.

'Monsieur,' he said, 'I've prepared rhubarb brioches and tea for you.' He might as well have said: *Monsieur, I've prepared some solace for you.*

Yes, I seek solace in food. And the more of it, the better. If I didn't have books as a source of consolation, I'd already look like the obese saddo who stalks my nightmares.

When I called my mother back, I'd barely said 'Hallo?' before she started crying and gasping for air.

'Maman, calm down, catch your breath, think of your blood pressure!' I shouted into my mobile.

'Even back in the bled, they know!' she wailed, repeating

the contents of her eleventh message. 'The whole family has heard about it! It's all over for me back there! I should rip up my passport right away! I'll never dare set foot in Algeria again! You can hide the truth, you can hide it for a long time, but the day it gets out it's big and it's bare!'

I asked to speak to Mina, on the basis that she'd adopt a calmer approach.

And yes, Mina was calm, serene even, as she said to me: 'If she was in front of me, I'd lynch her.'

The Bud that Destroys the Tree

The mystery has been solved. The famous Bernard T., to whom Dounia dedicated her autobiography, is none other than the former interior minister, Bernard Tartois. The rumours were doing the rounds before it was finally confirmed: they're an item. A pundit spilled the beans on the radio yesterday morning.

I bet Dounia's happy.

And I bet my mother now needs a new and long prescription.

Thank goodness she was still on a hundred percent. All medical expenses covered. What a blessing!

Tartois, from what I remember, was the sensation of the last government and the darling of the media. He was forever being featured on the glossy covers of *Gala, Paris-Match* and co. In the summer, there would be photos of him relaxing on the beach in his swim shorts.

His looks gave him a head start. Compared to other ministers at the time, he was Brad Pitt. I'm thinking of Regis Endeleau, for example, the former minister for foreign affairs, who was gangly and with the ruddy complexion of a newborn.

Tartois is the kind of guy who drools while speaking. When you watch him, the first thing you notice is his secretion problem.

Every time I landed on him during a televised political debate, I had to stop myself from throwing up. I couldn't help staring at his drool-filled mouth. I imagined him forgetting to swallow it one day, and spitting foam instead.

My sister Dounia was in a relationship with Bernard Tartois... Holy shit! Why?

My thoughts returned to my sobbing and wailing mother. I listened again to her message, which I'd carefully saved – even after listening to it thousands of times, it still had the same effect on me.

I decided to text my sister: *Bernard Tartois. Holy shit! Why?*

I'd gone into Miloud-mode, writing exactly what I thought. No tact, no pity. For once, it felt good to part ways with my politeness. She replied within the minute.

He makes me happy.

Our parents did their best to make *you* happy, Dounia, but that was never enough for you. And now you expect me to believe this big spittle-drooler-of-a-Tartois fills you with joy?

Tell me the truth, the one that hurts, big and bare, as Maman would say. Go on, admit it, given your unfettered ambition! You figured a former minister could do you no harm, didn't you, what with all the perks and his fat address book? Be honest, you enjoy that reflection of success. You love what you represent in the eyes of those people: the courageous daughter of immigrants, who started out with nothing and is now such a success story.

As for your book, the least I can say is you've bled the lexical battlefield dry. I highlighted in yellow all the times you used words such as *fighting... beaten... combat... struggle... battle...* Like any teacher worth their salt, I was this close to writing 'superflous' in red pen in the margins.

And when I think how I used to admire your gutsiness....

The truth is, you're not strong. Quite the opposite. You're weak. You're the weakest out of all of us.

'I wasn't made to be submissive', you write on page 47.

Well, we're all submissive, whether we like it or not. There are those who submit to God, with total and visible submission. And there are those who do so in spite of themselves, submitting to the laws of the financial markets, to the dictates of fashion, or to being loved.

You have become a rare kind of submissive, Dounia, in spite of yourself. The kind of submissive who thinks they're a rebel. And who seeks out other submissives to rescue.

It reminds me of a joke our grandfather, Sidi Ahmed Chennoun, used to tell, the one about the dromedary who mocks the dromedary in front for having a hump.

So yes, I've read your book, and it was dross. Badly written and pretentious. If you ask me, you're emulating Tartois the gobster: you spend your time spitting.

You spit on your parents, on Muslims, on Arabs, on marriage, on traditions, on yourself.

You spit on everything that makes you who you are.

You are the bud that destroys the trunk.

At the end of the book, you thank the Republic for inculcating you with its values. You claim that it nourished you. Well, judging by the results, it offered scant sustenance. And you reproach Maman for force-feeding you....

Your lack of gratitude disgusts me. The only word that comes to mind is: 'Tffffou!'

Despite the rift between the two of you, Maman loves you more than the Republic, and all the Tartois apparatchiks it produces, ever will.

Mehdi Mazouani

At school, aside from a few isolated incidents, I was making headway with my tough soviet line. My avatar of a heartless Vladimir, raised in the tundra by a pack of wolves, was proving a strong ally. Especially with my Year 9s.

I had finally met the notorious Mehdi Mazouani. He hadn't shown his face at school since the beginning of term.

Then the deputy head, Monsieur Diaz, pinned a message on the noticeboard: 'Mehdi Mazouani will be rejoining us at the end of October. Champagne.'

It didn't take me long to discover the reason for his sarcasm.

I asked Diaz where this student had been for the past two months.

'Look, his father's... one of a kind... so he sent his son back to the old country to *tighten a few loose screws*. Those are his words.'

At 15 and a half, Mehdi Mazouani is the oldest and tallest in his year group. When he walked into my class for the first time, he had a defiant look in his eye, a cigarette wedged behind one ear and the beginnings of a beard.

He sat at the back of the class, dumped his backpack on the table and started tagging with Tippex.

If you analyse where students choose to sit in class it can

lead to some highly deterministic conclusions. At one level, they're already choosing their standing in the world.

Luckily, there are always exceptions to the rule.

I asked the other students to recap what we'd studied so far. As usual, Sarah Zerdad, one of the front row faithfuls (and the big sister of Asma, the little asthmatic girl in my Year 7 class) was the first to raise her hand.

'We looked at how to construct an argument, sir!'

'Yes! And can you explain what an argument is?'

'An argument means explaining and giving evidence to support an idea...'

'Excellent, Sarah !'

Mehdi Mazouani raised his eyebrows without bothering to glance up from his Tippex work of art.

As long as he doesn't disturb my lesson, I thought, but realised how cowardly I was being. So I went for it.

'Mehdi, we're re-capping on the lessons for your benefit. Please sit appropriately, put your bag on the floor and take off your jacket!'

He did as he was told, without batting an eyelid.

Once he was sitting properly, he broke into a sneer. 'Like, do I even givva-shit? This is bare long, innit.'

Armoured vehicle. Tank. Armoured vehicle.

'Kindly change your tone of voice when speaking to me.'

'Why? Who even *are* you man? What's your life to me, wesh? You aint my dad, innit, so don't talk to me, yeah.'

'I'm your French teacher and you're to speak to me with respect, is that clear? To start with, you should be addressing me as 'Sir'!'

'Or what? You think I'm scared of you? Come outta my way, man, like it's not so deep.'

'If you continue like that, I'll have to report you to the Head.'

'Go on then! These roolz are wack anyway, innit? Like 'low it, man, I swear. Do I even givva-shit?'

He was making chewing-gum out of the words 'givva-shit'.

'Don't bust my balls, wesh. I'm here already, innit. Tfffff. Who are yoouuu, fam?! Raaaah, I swear, is this guy for real?'

Immodium. Immodium. Immodium.

I'd have given anything for a talented film director to intervene.

Cut! CUT! We'll do a retake, okay! This isn't working, kiddos, let's try again! Mourad, sweetie, I didn't believe in you! Stand your ground, be authoritative! We need to sense you holding it together – you were too fragile there, lovey... Right, let's go again, and this time show us your tough side. All right, poppet? You've got to be a wall, I want a wall in front of me! That's the idea! Think Berlin Wall, think breeze-blocks, think bricks and mortar, okay? Mehdi, darling, perfect, don't change a thing, so raw, the tough kid with no scruples... genius! Do exactly the same again, I love the emotion you're giving it! Make-up, can we powder a few faces before they start going shiny! Thank you! Right! Can someone get me a coffee, for fuck's sake?! I've been asking for the past hour! Where did that intern go...? What's his name again? Amadou? Amadi? Kid like that should jump at an opportunity like this. All right, everyone ready? Let's go! Lights... Camera... Action !

But Mehdi carried on tagging his backpack with his wretched Tippex tube that was at the end of its life, squeezing it every which way to extract the final drops.

While the other students were enjoying the show, I was picturing them turning their thumbs down to signal I should be put to death.

'You'll stay behind at the end of class, Mehdi, I'd like a word with you in private.'

'Yeah, yeah... whatevva... like do I even givva-shit?'

Sarah's eyes, big and shiny as two moons, met mine. In them, I read the despair of the good student. I recognised her exasperation at having-it-up-to-here. My own eyes were filled with that feeling too, at the same age.

I tried to finish off my lesson as best I could by ignoring Mehdi's multiple provocations.

Aladji, one of the jokers in the middle rows, read out a text about a sailing resort. He said 'yacked' instead of 'yacht', which got a laugh from the five intellects in the class.

When the bell finally rang, it boomed inside my ribcage in Dolby surround sound.

The students filed out of the classroom in clusters of twos and threes.

As for Mehdi Mazouani, he stood out as a lone wolf. They're an odd species but I can spot them straight away. I'm similar, but in the lamb version.

Of course, he made a show of leaving. He walked slowly, knowing I'd call him back, banking on it even.

'Mehdi, you're staying with me for a minute!'

He was staring indifferently at his fingers, which were covered in Tippex.

'I'll level with you: I don't want to carry on like this for the rest of the year.'

'True dat. Don't wanna be here neither.'

'Really? So you want to leave school?'

'Yeah, fam. This place does my head in.'

'What *do* you want to do?'

'Dunno. Man aint decided yet.'

'Well, I think it's stupid.'

'You calling me stupid?'

'I think it's stupid throwing your life away like this.'

'Like do I even givva-shit? S'cool, my life's trashed, wesh.'

'What makes you say that? You're only 15!'

'You for real, sir, with all the questions?'

His use of 'sir' hadn't slipped my notice.

'Yes, I'm for real.'

'You blatantly have not met my old man.'

'No, I haven't yet had that pleasure.'

Pleasure? Raaah! I'm not here to tell you my lifestory, you get me. So, you gonna rat on me, or what? I've seen the bigman four times since Monday so, like, do I even givva-shit?

'No, I'm not going to report you, but we're going to make a pact, you and I. You may not want to be here, but plenty of students *are* keen to attend my lessons. So from now on I want you to behave calmly in my classroom, please, and then I won't ask too much of you.'

'Yeah, yeah, calm.'

'Agreed? Can I count on you?'

'It's caaaalm, man. Hey, your whip gets ratings! C Class, sir! Leather seats! That is claaass.'

I thought of the expression, 'Necessity knows no law'.

If I ask the minimum of him, and this leads to peace, perhaps he'll want to give a bit more?

We'll see what happens, I reflected, *but for now... like do I even givva-shit?*

Stand By Me

Hélène had invited me over to dinner at hers.

'Are you familiar with the centre of Aubervilliers?'

Not exactly. I mean, it was the banlieue, right?

I was reacting like someone born and bred in the 16th arrondissement.

This marked the second time in my life that a girl had asked me out.

The first time was the last night party of our school ski trip. My primary school teacher, Monsieur Mounier, had persuaded a girl in my class called Rita to do a slow dance with me.

'Come on, Rita!' he'd said. 'Be nice! Go and ask him! He's shy!

'Naaaaah, not *him*...! Embarrassing or what? He's a homesick cry-baby, sir, he doesn't even know how to ski! He's scared of falling into a hole!'

We danced the slow together, but you can bet Rita didn't look at me, not once. All she did was puff out her cheeks and sigh. It was *Stand By Me* by Ben E. King. Sighing should be banned during *Stand By Me*.

Unfortunately, Hélène wasn't planning a romantic date for the two of us, but a relaxed dinner for a few of the teachers.

The 'nice bunch' having a get-together. I wasn't sure if she counted Gérard as 'nice', and I hadn't pressed for further details, but I decided to buy chocolates and flowers anyway. Hélène had texted me her address. 'Remember, work is off-limits!' she added, cheekily.

I arrived early, like those social misfits who turn up at 7.30 'to lend a hand' even though you invited them for 8pm. The truth was, I was hoping for some quality time with la belle Hélène.

But I hadn't factored in Gérard, the monster social misfit, who must have turned up at 7.20. He was already sitting on the sofa, champagne glass in hand.

Hélène gave me a peck on both cheeks, and it felt a bit like when old ladies who still wear make-up leave the traces of their crime, in the form of pink smears, on the faces of young kids.

'Wow! Flowers! I'm being spoiled! They're gorgeous! And what's that? Chocolate? Heck, Mourad! My diet!'

She was laughing.

'Gérard's already here. Go on, make yourself comfy. What can I pour you?'

'Water, please.'

Obviously, I took off my shoes, which left me completely out of breath. Like a post-coital rabbit.

'Hey, so it's the boy from Nice! It wasn't too complicated for you finding this place?' asked Gérard.

He'd started up again with his stupid questions.

Hélène's apartment was cute as a button. On the sitting room table was a lilac tablecloth, candy pink curtains at the windows, candles everywhere and little bronze Buddhas. Naturally, the bookshelves were crammed to overflowing with books, most of them in English editions.

I was already under Hélène's spell, but I fell in love with her the moment I saw her bookshelves.

Gérard polished off his glass.

'Adorable place, right?'

'Yes, very.'

'Is this your first time here?'

'Yes. What about you?'

'Oh, no, no, no...'

He said 'no, no, no' with a knowing air.

You'd think he was about to give me a guided tour or show me where the toilets were. He was clearly making the point that he had been enjoying privileged access for some time. Who did he take himself for? The landlord?

Caroline, the thin-lipped art teacher, arrived, followed by Wilfried, the long-term supply teacher, Claude, the History and Geography teacher, Sabine, Head of Year, and Simon Moulin, the Music teacher.

They all kept their shoes on. I felt stupid in my sports socks.

Claude opened the hostilities with his 'dumbing down' debate.

'I'm sorry, but we're not here to do the parents' job for them! Adopting a social worker approach means dumbing down our subjects. It's not our job to raise those kids. I waste a crazy amount of time asking them to be quiet, to sit properly, to calm down. And when I'm not doing that, I'm filling out student disciplinary action forms, sorting out their quarrels and sending code of conduct letters to their parents!'

'It always comes back to this!' sighed Hélène. 'Of course we're not paid to do the parents' job for them... but discipline *is* part of the deal, Claude! Remember, they're 14, they're only kids, after all... They need us to help establish boundaries, and it's only normal we should do that! Right, Gérard?'

"Authority's innate, you've either got it or you haven't – that's my take on it! No need to keep proving you're strong. If the kids sense you're the strongest, they'll respect you. There's no secret method.'

'All right, but we're not in a gulag either, so outbursts are inevitable... Sorry, but we all know the torture of the last lesson on a Friday afternoon. They're over-excited, and so are we. Everyone's exhausted, it's the end of the week, and we all want out – they're not stupid, they sense it.... As far as I'm concerned, it's a pointless hour in the timetable, I'm just marking time, if I'm honest!'

Caroline listened carefully and her cheeks turned red as she ate her salad.

'I'm with you, Hélène,' she declared, putting her fork down. 'The hardline disciplinarian approach doesn't do it for me. I think we can be sensitive to their anger, to how tired they're feeling, to their personal problems, and we can be respected for doing so. They understand that we're helping them to establish boundaries.... Quite a few of my students stay behind at the end of my lessons, to have a chat, to confide in me...'

'Sure, and that's why you miss all your breaks! You're not the school counsellor, you know!'

'No, Gérard, I'm not the school counsellor, but we need to engage at this level! What role are teachers meant to play today? More is being asked of us, for sure. But it's not just about beating them over the head with learning objectives!'

'That's easy enough for you to say! You toss some paper and a box of coloured pencils their way, they draw you a rainbow, and you can go home happy, job done.'

There was a general protest of 'Woooaaah!'

'That was out of order! What's with knocking creative subjects?' asked Simon the Music teacher. 'I thought we were done with woolly thinking! Creativity is essential for personal development, and you know it! We're opening their minds.'

'Spot-on! Contrary to what you may think, Gérard, I don't just 'toss' them a box of coloured pencils every lesson. And yes, of course I find it rewarding to talk to them about Kandinsky, and get them out of Montreuil to visit an art gallery or a museum. You do realise most of them have never set foot in one? They've got no idea what an exhibition is!'

'Those parents couldn't care less about their kids going to exhibitions! They want us to teach them how to read and count! End of! If we manage to cover the curriculum basics, that's already a result! So my point is... if getting them to listen to rap in their lessons isn't dumbing down, Simon, I don't know what it is!'

'Why wouldn't I get them to listen to rap? Encouraging them to approach it differently, and to analyse the music rigorously, is highly beneficial. And if I were teaching in the centre of Paris, I'd do exactly the same!'

'So what kind of deeper analsyis do you recommend for *Nique ta race, bitch?*! Are you calling that music?'

'There you go! Wham-bam! The usual clichés about rap! You remind me of my grandfather who used to tell my dad that rock wasn't music! Stop playing the old fogey! It doesn't suit you.'

Personally, I thought it fitted Gérard like a glove.

Claude picked up the conversation and his wine glass too.

'It's true, for fuck's sake! Where's the sense? We make promises we can't deliver on... I've been teaching in the 93 postcode for 20 years and, let me tell you, I've seen reform after reform implemented, but I haven't witnessed a single miracle! My former students, and I'm talking the lucky ones here, are either Carrefour megastore security guards, or sports shop retail assistants! While the girls are receptionists, if they're easy enough on the eye. And I'm not even talking about the ones I see hanging out at the PMU on rue de Paris all day long, blowing their benefits on scratchcards and Rapido down the betting shop!'

Hélène stood up and brought over the roast chicken.

'Right, gathering of the great disillusioned, are we done with our 15 minutes' worth? Wilfried, can you carve, please?'

I ate in silence, frightened someone might ask me for my view.

Naturally, Gérard was in no mood to spare me.

'What about you, new kid on the block! What's your view, eh, seeing as you've just started out? Landed with a bump?'

'Er... not really. I went in with no prior knowledge, and I'm learning on the job. I don't subscribe to a particular method, I just try to keep an open mind and to work with what I've got.'

'So you're going with the flow, right? You're improvising?'

'A bit, yes, of course. I don't have any choice. There are days when I walk into my classroom and I feel like a lion-tamer entering the cage. Something's playing out between them, you have to go with your instincts...'

'Ha ha! That's a good one! The lion tamer theory! Haven't heard that before! Then again, I'm all for bringing back the cane...'

Sabine, Head of Year, raised an eyebrow at Gérard.

'What are you playing at, Gégé? What's with this reactionary 'back to basics' stuff?'

'It's not reactionary! Excuse me, but I've clocked up 25 years of teaching experience here!'

'Bloody hell, you communists all age so badly!'

Everyone laughed, except Gérard, who poured himself

another glass of wine. He was more frustrated than me and, let me tell you, it takes some doing to beat a virgin of my age in the frustration stakes.

Hélène served up the chicken and suggested we *switch topics*. Everyone appeared to agree.

'Have you heard about Emilie Boulanger?'

'That mousey kid with the big boobs in Year 8?

'Why? What's up with her?'

'She's got a bun in the oven! I had a meeting with her mum this afternoon...'

'Emilie Boulanger! But she's only *13*!'

'You're kidding? When do they start these days? In Year 4?'

'These are the times we're in! Get with the programme!'

'That said, the poor kid was already a 34B last year!'

'You'll see why if you meet the mum! The lights are but no one's at home!'

'Sabine, that's cruel!'

'What a bunch of gossips we are!'

They clucked like hens, and it wouldn't have taken much for them to start laying eggs.

I concluded that the only reason teachers chose to work in secondary schools was out of nostalgia for when they were 14.

I was the last person to leave Hélène's apartment.

'You in a hurry?' she asked.

I was struggling to put on my pair of electric-blue All Stars, with my head pressed against the hallway wall.

'Well, er, yes, kind of... I... er...it's a bit of a journey.'

'Sure thing, too bad I guess.... Good night, Mourad, and thanks for the flowers....'

How much of a saddo can I be?

But it was Hélène's fault, too! What had come over her, suddenly inviting me to stay on like that? She'd looked sort of flirtatious and her voice had sounded husky. I mean, it's not like I give off a Casanova vibe. So what's with scaring a celibate young man? That flirty voice was a bad idea, I've never felt so blocked in all my life.

I was so angry with myself I felt like slamming my head against a wall until my brains spilled out.

Miloud would have been in there like a shot. Staying over is more his style; lounging about the apartment the next morning in his underwear and eating the remains of the cold chicken for breakfast.

With all the wisdom of his 15 years, Mehdi Mazouani wouldn't have held back either. *Wesh wesh, I'm in no rush! I aint got nuttin' else to do, you get me. Why don't you strip off dem trousers, yeah? You were bare on it, like a jezzy – proper leadin' me on an' dat, so show man how it's done – cos I aint gonna bust my balls.* The truth is, anybody else would have seized the occasion.

I needed to walk off the embarrassment. Wafts of urine and roasted chestnuts rose up from the métro, hanging in the night air of Aubervilliers. A few men were smoking in front of a bar and speaking in Arabic: it could have been one of those Egyptian films from the 1970's, where the actresses wake up in the morning with their faces already heavily made-up. My mother can't get enough of them.

A Chinese working-girl was leaning against a bollard in front of a Western Union branch. Behind her was a poster of a young Indian girl writing in her school exercise book. Underneath the photo: *Uniting people with possibilities: the fastest way to send money – worldwide.*

If I'd had the guts, I'd have gone over to that sad Chinese

girl with her bandy legs planted in the tarmac. I'd have asked if she was all right and she probably wouldn't have answered me, just named her price, miming with her hands as she stared into the distance, a worried look in her eyes, as if she were being watched from the other side of the main road.

I'd follow her into the first sleazy hotel. The stairwell would smell rank, of vinegar maybe. She'd climb the stairs two at a time with those bandy legs, and in the bedroom she'd take off her fake rabbit fur jacket, followed by her lace blouse. In spite of everything, and even though I'd be thinking of Hélène and keeping my eyes shut tight, I wouldn't be able to do it.

After a few minutes, the Chinese girl, bored of waiting half-naked, while I sat on the mattress with my failed manhood, would offer up a few insults in her language as she got dressed again, before heading out and leaving me there like a prize moron.

In the cold Aubervilliers night, the working-girl with bandy legs kept staring into the distance, gazing at some invisible point. Perhaps she was having painful thoughts about everything she'd left behind in her province of Liaoning, about her ailing parents, or her scarcely-weaned infant.... Yes, thinking about it, she looked over 30. Was she a mother already? Just the thought made me feel ashamed, I don't like mixing categories. Have I got a problem?

I flanked the walls and corrugated iron hoardings where a few notices had been fly-posted.

Marcel Désiré Bijou, eminent preacher of Kinshasa, promises to deliver the secret of eternal light, on Sunday 6th December at three o'clock, in the Evangelical Lutheran Church of Absolute Faith, in Nanterre.

With a name like that, Marcel Désiré Bijou must have a mother who's even more overbearing than mine.

What with his sharp suit in white and mauve, teamed with a matching hat, I was picturing his umbilical cord in real leather or solid gold.

Why lie about it? My mother would never appreciate a girl like Hélène. Just as she'd never appreciate any other girl either. At that price, I might as well get castrated. With a bit of luck I'd be taken on as a eunarch in a Turkish hammam.

The light in the grand living room was on when I arrived back at Liliane's. Had Mario forgotten to turn off the lights? *Impossible,* I thought, *Mario never makes a single mistake*!

It was almost 2am and I found Liliane, in her green satin dressing gown, reduced to tears in front of the large mirror above the mantelpiece. She kept touching her face, as if checking everything was still in the right place.

'What's the matter, Liliane? Is something wrong?'

'I'm having regrets, Mourad! I should never have gone ahead with this! I can barely smile! And my expression is one of permanent astonishment! I look ghastly!'

'You *so* don't look ghastly! Please, don't worry! Remember what the surgeon said, it will all settle down with time. Your skin will relax. Just like the leather on new shoes.'

'The leather on new shoes?!'

'Sorry, Liliane, it's the first example that came to mind. You have to remember my father's a cobbler... Where's Miloud?'

'Miloud's asleep. He's sleeping peacefully, with his whole life ahead of him. Why would he lumber himself with a silly old goose like me?'

'Don't talk like that! You know Miloud's crazy about you.'

Is that what's called a white lie?

'Please, Mourad! I'm not as naïve as I look! I know he

loves me, but the way he would a mother. Because, guess what, I'm exactly the same age as his mother!'

That didn't help me any.

'I should have listened to him! He told me not to meddle with my face! What's my son going to say? Edouard's coming to Paris shortly! He's taken a few days off for Thanksgiving.'

'That's great news! How long has it been since his last visit?'

'If I'm doing the maths right, we haven't seen each other for six years. Can you imagine, Mourad? Six years? The only proof I have that he's alive is that automatic bank transfer.... If you knew what he shakes me down for each month. It's scandalous! I can see the words 'daylight robbery' in my accountant's eyes. I'm just a cash cow with a facelift.'

I felt distinctly awkward. I'd been staying rent-free at Liliane's for nearly three months now.

'Don't look at me like that! I'm not talking about you! I'm talking about my own son, who doesn't even deign to ring me on my birthday! I know he holds it against me for leaving his father! Children are horrible! They're so selfish!'

'Don't think about it any more! It's late, you should get some rest.'

'Rest? If only! I've taken two Stilnox - and I still can't catch a wink of sleep! It doesn't have any effect on me any more! My body's too used to hypnotics... Tell me something, Mourad?'

'Yes ?

'Would you mind staying with me for a little while? I get terribly anxious at night, you know.'

'Of course, no worries, I'll stay with you, Liliane. We can talk about it, if you'd like.'

'Let me tell you something, I don't think anybody's ever truly loved me, or at least not in the right way.'

We sat together on the couch.

I held her hand and she talked about her unfaithful ex-husband, about her mother who was so perfect, about her absent father and the great-uncle with the house in the Champagne region where she and her sister Violette used to spend their holidays. He would insist on giving them a bath, even when they were12 and 14. The tears poured down the taut skin of Liliane's face.

As night falls, so too do people's masks.

Tsunami

My worst nightmare, after the one about the obese saddo with salt-and-pepper hair, involves a tsunami at the end of time.

I'm on a beach, which is outrageously beautiful and deserted. The sea looks calm. As I stroll along, I'm fretting about whether the damp sand between my toes will create a mess in the hallway.

I can already picture my mother making a song and dance about it and shaking her bottle of bleach at me. 'What d'you take me for?' she'll complain. 'A skivvy? A slave? Do you want to watch me dying with a mop in my hands?!'

I try to put those thoughts out of my head and I keep on walking. I can see someone in the distance: it's Big Baba, and he's waving at me. As I draw nearer, I realise he's in a wheelchair which has sunk into the sand.

'Mourad, help me!' Big Baba implores. 'Have pity on me! I'm stuck!'

I push with all my strength, but there's no dislodging the wheelchair. Down on my knees, I dig around the wheels. I can feel the sand wedging itself under my nails. Nothing shifts. It's as if the contraption is bolted into the ground. Big Baba is begging me to rescue him but, despite all my efforts, the wheelchair won't budge a millimetre. My chest crumples with anxiety as the sobs rise up inside me. I want to cry.

There's no escaping my emotions, and so I cry a flood of tears salty as seawater.

'No!!! No!!!' Big Baba is shouting now. 'Don't cry! Don't do that! Men don't cry!'

And then I hear a dull rumbling, a terrible noise, the sound of the famished earth opening up its belly, preparing to swallow everything. I turn around and see the towering wave – it's so high, so rapid.

My father bellows.

He bellows and I cry, the wheels of the wheelchair are stuck in the sand, the wave is coming straight for us.

Babar Syndrome

I used to adore the stories of Babar the elephant. They cradled my childhood. I even read them to Big Baba at bedtime.

Not the other way around.

Mina had called me earlier in the day to find out what I planned to do with my book collection. She and Jalil were clearing out Big Baba's sheds in the garden.

'Papa's got so much stuff! It's unbelievable! I can't get over the junk I've found!'

'Like what?'

'Like a rusty pneumatic drill, a tractor tyre, a blow-up Perrier bottle, a javelin, 55 metres of rope and at least 20 Beatles records! I mean, come again? The Beatles! Since when was Papa into the Beatles?'

I don't think he had ever listened to the Beatles. He must have found all that vinyl somewhere, scooped it up and dumped it in the shed, along with everything else.

'And, wait for it! Every pair of shoes from his shop! The shed's full to bursting with them!'

Big Baba enjoyed a special relationship with what he referred to as the 'orphans': occasionally, customers would drop off their shoes never to reclaim them. Our father stockpiled these abandoned pairs on the basis that their owners might one day re-appear. The result was an outsize orphanage of clodhoppers in the wooden shed at the end of the garden.

'So, Mourad, back to your books from when you were little. What are we doing with them? There's all your *Babars*...'

'Don't throw them out, whatever you do! They're very special to me!'

'Fine, but what d'you want me to do with them?'

'Why don't you rescue them for your own children?'

'Not on my watch! Never!'

'How come?'

'Because *Babar* is just a story to glorify colonialism... I'm not reading that to my kids!'

'You and your theories, Mina! Aren't you going a bit far?'

'Really? An old white lady who teaches an elephant how to behave in polite society? From one day to the next, he starts walking on two legs, wearing three-piece suits and driving a car, so he can return to the jungle and foist his new way of life upon his entire tribe of elephants... What would you call it, then?'

Viewed from that angle, her argument held up.

'How's Papa doing?'

'Hamdoullah. He's doing okay. They're trying to get him to walk now, with the walking frame.'

'Good. That's progress.'

'But you know what he's like... Always moaning. He keeps saying things like: 'It's too much for me' or 'Leave me in peace'. All he wants to do is eat, sleep and mope. He's desperate to get out of hospital, he's had it with that place. Oh, and he keeps saying how much he misses his cat.'

'What cat?'

'Who knows? Maybe he's talking about Moustico, the

neighbour's cat.'

'So where are we at with getting permission for him to leave hospital?'

'His doctor hasn't got back to us yet. It'll only be for a weekend, in any case. But it might help motivate him. How about you? When are you coming back? Have you bought your tickets yet?'

'You bet. Eight days to go 'til the end of term!'

'I'm telling you, start starving yourself – Maman's made your favourite cakes, as well as her makrouts and griwechs.'

My mother would be offended if she found out that I'd developed a taste for Mario's delicious rhubarb brioches over her Algerian cookies and fritters.

I couldn't wait to return to Nice. It was as if ten years had gone by.

At school, things were back to normal with Hélène, at least on the face of it. But there was still something niggling me, like a small stone in my shoe. I noticed she didn't smile at me so often, and that she spent all her breaks with Gérard, who openly taunted me.

At the IUFM, they kept assaulting us with gobbledygook about teaching, woolly concepts and some abstract guff about knowledge transfer, all of which bored me to tears.

Why didn't anyone talk to us about boys like Mehdi Mazouani, where the only thing keeping them at school was the threat of being sent back to the bled? Or girls like Emilie Boulanger, who jacked in their education when they found themselves pregnant at 13, before they'd even labelled a diagram of a uterus in a biology lesson? And why didn't they explain how to go about cutting a rough diamond like Sarah Zerdad, without her becoming demoralised and losing her sparkle?

On the subject of Mehdi Mazouani, I'd heard from some of the students that he'd been badly beaten up by a gang of youths at Maraîchers station. I was worried about him, to be honest I was fond of the kid, and yes, I even did givva-shit. I pictured him, trying to force back his tears, the bitter taste of blood filling his mouth.

I wondered if his father would show up at parents' evening. I was very curious to meet him, just as I was curious about meeting the parents of my other students. It would be an occasion to put to the test that old proverb, 'the fruit never falls far from the tree'.

Big Baba had never missed a parents' evening, not once.

'How is it that you never get into trouble for talking in class?' he had asked me one day.

'Nobody wants to talk to me.'

Dounia had been trying to get in touch. I was deliberately avoiding her. We were supposed to be travelling to Nice together, during the school holidays, so she could visit Big Baba in hospital, but I'd already bought my ticket.

Back at Liliane's after a day's teaching, I finally decided to listen to my voicemails.

Dounia has this irritating habit of starting her messages with: 'Hi, it's Dounia, we're Tuesday, it's a tad after four...', or 'Hey Mourad, it's Dounia, Thursday, and it's a tad before 9am. ...'.

How annoying is that? Firstly, it's pointless, because the voicemail automatically gives you the date and time, and secondly, no one's said 'tad' since at least the mid-Eighties.

She was talking about some dinner being held the following evening at the Swedish embassy. It was in honour of the Swedish minister for immigration and integration who was on an official visit to Paris. My sister, as part of the French delegation, was cordially inviting me to join them.

I know it's silly, but I couldn't help thinking of those ads for Ferrero Rocher: '*The ambassador's receptions are noted in society for their host's exquisite taste, that captivates his guests…*'

The voiceover was followed by suggestive music and an elegant Chinese guest biting into the crunchy chocolate-coating before exclaiming: '*Delicious!*'

I was convinced Dounia had an ulterior motive. And that ulterior motive doubtless involved a centre-right dynamic 40-something with over-productive salivary glands. Knowing her, she'd found the dream occasion to introduce me to Bernard Tartois, the man who *made her happy*.

'Next weekend, I'm free to visit Papa in Nice,' her message went on, 'if that still works for you...'

I can't deny that Dounia's got balls.

Good to know, at least *she's* got them.

I showered and borrowed some clothes from Miloud, who's always thrilled to show off his Armani suits, Dior jeans and patent leather Weston shoes.

I don't think I'd ever been so smart and presentable.

'I swear, you're looking the part, cuz! Saha! I'll drop you off, if you like! I'm taking Liliane out tonight cos she's feeling down...'

I smiled at Miloud, who was dripping with the effort of putting on such a show.

'What's with the eligible bachelor act, Miloud! Why don't you 'fess up to *her* being the one taking *you* out!'

Miloud and Liliane dropped me off at rue Barbet-de-Jouy, in the 7th arrondissement. Dounia came to welcome me at the metal gates, wearing a sophisticated trouser suit and 15cm heels, minimum. Which made giving her a peck on the cheek an odd experience.

Anyway, she seemed relieved to see me.

'I was worried you might be a no-show...' she whispered.

Which is exactly what *should* have happened.

I thought of Big Baba and what he'd said back in the summer when he had asked to see Dounia. I owed it to him to respect his wishes, or risk feeling like a bad son for the rest of my days. Make that *an even worse son*.

There were already about 15 guests in the ultra-chic reception room, holding on tight to their wine glasses. Everybody had formed a natural circle around the minister, and they nodded while listening to him religiously, as if participating in some kind of occult ceremony.

But the person leading the ceremony was neither long in the tooth nor an obscure guru. Mr. Erik Ullenstrass, the Swedish minister for immigration and integration, was young and handsome and apparently very witty, because whenever he opened his mouth everybody split their sides.

Sadly, my level of English wasn't up to laughing. *Pity about Hélène,* I mused. *I've missed out on private English lessons too.*

Dounia led me by the arm to the west side of the circle.

I recognised Tartois, who greeted me with his politician's smile while modelling a firm and frank handshake, exactly the way he'd been taught.

He was in 'Bernard's-out-campaigning' mode: the fish market in Saint-François, say, on a Sunday morning, before the second round of presidential elections. He was this close to handing me a leaflet and urging: 'Vote for me!'

Holy shit. I already regretted accepting the invitation.

One of the Cambodian waiters wore spotless white gloves, stood bolt upright and glided with quick, tiny steps: a carbon copy of Mario, albeit one that smiled more readily. He held out a silver tray arrayed with champagne glasses. I considered those tiny bubbles rising to the surface, like so many Bulgarian working-girls surfacing along the promenade des Anglais, in Nice's red-light district.

'No. Thank you,' I managed in English. I didn't dare ask for anything else, even though my throat was so dry and tickly I was about to start coughing up dust.

While the guests were bidden by the ambassador to make their way towards the dining room, another waiter held out another tray, this time arrayed with tiny wooden sculptures bearing guest cards. When I spotted the words 'Mourad Chennoun', I instinctively reached out.

'That'll be my one,' I muttered under my breath. The Cambodian waiter subtly averted my hand, shaking his head and smiling politely.

'That's the table plan, Mourad,' Dounia whispered in my ear, coming to the rescue. 'It's just so you know where to sit....'

Talk about humiliating. I felt like something out of la Fontaine's *The Town Mouse and the Country Mouse.*

What would Mehdi Mazouani have said? *You for real, my Made-in-Taiwan breddah, with your 3D table plan*? *'Low it, fam! Man's sittin' where I want, you get me? Like, do I even givva-shit?*

Moments like these are a classic trigger for my laxophobia.

Imodium. Imodium. Imodium.

Luckily, I've always got some on me.

The guests were mostly top brass, but also included the director of a charity supporting ex-offenders to reintegrate into society, as well as a young newspaper journalist with strong BO. They looked as out of place as I did. And that's factoring in my head start with the knives and forks, thanks to the number of posh dinner parties thrown by Liliane.

Everyone had introduced themselves and now it was my turn.

'I'm a secondary school French teacher in a ZEP, meaning an educational priority zone, in Montreuil.' It felt like justifying being there. Trying to save face.

On my right, a plump blond woman shook with nerves as she explained her job. I gleaned that it had something to do with sociology, ethnology and statistics, and that she published essays, the most recent being *The Failure of Assimilation*.

The young journalist with smelly armpits made a brief presentation. He wrote for the education section of a major daily, which was all he told us, apart from his name. He seemed more interested in what was on his plate. If my mother had been a guest at the table, she'd have told him: 'Hey! You there! Easy does it! Anyone would think you'd never seen food before in your life! Born in a barn, were you? Makhlouh!'

Erik Ullenstrass narrowed his blue eyes and stroked his chin with his thumb and index finger as he listened to his guests, nodding occasionally. A female assistant was translating everything into Swedish for him, while affording us a view of her nostrils.

Tartois began to speak. At length. Considerable length.

He went on for long enough to produce litres and litres of drool, enough gob and spittle to drown out an entire continent.

'So, in your view,' Erik Ullenstrass inquired in English, 'is the French model of integration in trouble?'

Tartois came straight back at him, adopting the expression of someone deeply concerned by the issue: 'Let's be absolutely clear about this, we are currently experiencing an unprecedented crisis of identity!'

Next, he gave us a 15-minute-whistle-stop-tour of the last five years' worth of current affairs. He talked about certain communities struggling to assimilate, about Muslims praying in the street, about linguistic impoverishment in the banlieues, about the veil in schools, about isolationism.

He mixed his cocktail with beguiling ease, like Tom Cruise, in you know which movie, back in the day.

Dounia was nodding and gazing at him adoringly.

I recalled my first lesson with my Year 7s, the one where I was explaining to them what a cliché was. From listening to Tartois-the-gobster, I was revising my opinion: if you want to succeed professionally, it turns out it's not strictly necessary to spot the clichés..

I'm not sure what came over me, but I interrupted his speechmaking.

'So, just to recap here, Bernard, France has a problem with Islam?'

Tartois eyeballed me and gulped, as in swallowed his drool for the first time since August 1977. He was staring at the guests, like a kid caught red-handed.

'No, no, now listen... that's *not* what I said! Far from it! No, that's absolutely *not* what I'm saying! Put simply, I'm a strong believer in secularism, and we need to recognise that it's more difficult for certain communities to adopt the French way of life, it seems to me, than it is for others.... In certain situations, there are traditions and practices which appear to be wholly incompatible with our secular Republic. We have to recognise this is the reality and open our eyes. It's our job both to acknowledge this and to put forward solutions.'

'Incompatible?'

As incompatible as you and my sister, for example?

Dounia jumped to the defence of her Bernie-kins.

'Come on, you're not seriously accusing Bernard of Islamophobia, just because he acknowledges this? Or saying that he's someone who doesn't respect personal freedoms?'

'Whose freedoms are we talking about?'

'Oh, please! Don't try that with me! I fight for women's freedom, in particular those women held hostage by an archaic patriarchal system which has no place in this country! Banning the veil in schools, for example, seems to me entirely justified! I can't begin to imagine why that would be challenged today!'

Even the journalist with smelly armpits had ditched his fork to follow our debate. The minister's and ambassador's eyes were sparkling, and the translator was stepping up her efforts so as not to miss anything.

I could feel my blood boiling.

'That's because you've got a personal problem with the veil!'

'Absolutely not! I have a personal problem with anyone who gets in the way of women being free!'

'But that's precisely what you're doing by banning the veil at school! You can't say to people: 'Be free OUR way, there's only one way to be free, and it's our way!' That's an absurd idea! And it doesn't work! It creates resentment and injustice! You say you're defending women, but what about the number of girls who've quit school because of this law?! They've drawn a line through all their ambitions, as well as through their only chance of escaping this archaic system you claim to be fighting...'

'No one's talking about imposing anything,' declared Bernard Tartois, crossing his arms, and staring at the ceiling. 'It's about everybody abiding by the same rules. It's about preventing a situation whereby, because of this insularity, because of this identity crisis we've been talking about, Dounias and Mourads are unable to feel French, to flourish and to contribute to the enrichment of this country.'

'What do you mean by "Dounias and Mourads"?'

'Er... Well, if we can put aside our personal paranoia for one moment, it's just a way of saying that we have to avoid isolationism at all costs, whatever people's social or ethnic origins...'

'I don't agree. And no, it's not *whatever* their origins, seeing as you've just highlighted our heritage in front of everybody...'

'So, what are you trying to say, Mourad?' my sister wanted to know.

'Yes, what's the problem? I don't see what's so shocking in any of this!'

'It's the contradiction I find shocking... I mean, to be fully French, you have to deny part of your heritage, part of your identity, part of your history, part of your beliefs, and yet even when you succeed in achieving all of that, you're still endlessly reminded of your origins.... So what's the point?'

Dounia was frowning. She didn't appear to share my view at all. As for her Tartois, I had got under his skin and now he was secreting ministerial drool. Yves Michonneau, the guy responsible for reintegrating ex-offenders, and who I'd warmed to instantly because he mopped up the gravy on his plate with his bread, spoke out.

'I totally hear what Mourad's trying to say. These are exactly the kind of remarks we come across in our organisation. Ex-offenders constantly feel side-lined and, as a result, they feel less and less motivated, well it's the same principle, isn't it...?'

My sister was sulking.

I think the poster boy minister was fired up by our exchange, because he kept whispering things in Swedish to the ambassador. Up until then, maybe he'd thought his trip to Paris wouldn't amount to much more than buying lingerie and French perfume for his wife.

Bernard Tartois put his hand on my arm. He meant it as a brotherly gesture, but I found it patronising. Was I being paranoid?

'What I said was in no way intended as a judgement, I think it's marvellous to exceed the limits imposed by the clan. Take Dounia, she offers an extraordinary example, and not just for you, but for all those younger brothers and sisters who'll look up to her and think: "She looks like me, she *is* like me, I too can succeed!"'

I smiled and politely removed Tartois's hand by taking hold of his wrist.

'Bernard? Are you familiar with *Babar, King of the Elephants*?'

'... Yes... And your point is?'

'It doesn't matter that Babar can walk on two legs, that he wears a three-piece suit and a bowtie, or that he drives an open-top car, he will always be an elephant!'

Tartois half-smiled.

Dounia was typing nervously on her Blackberry, texting under the table.

'The Minister wonders whether perhaps, having only read *The Adventures of Babar* in Swedish translation, he may have missed something,' queried the ambassador.

I kept quiet until coffee.

Tartois continued to proffer his opinion on every topic, through a suspension of spittle.

'Fancy joining me outside? I'm going for a smoke,' Dounia asked me after the meal.

I nodded and followed my big sister as she strolled ahead in her high heels, clutching the Philip Morris packet in her left hand and her Blackberry in the right.

In the courtyard, her fulsome lips pinched the filter tightly, but the flame from the lighter kept sputtering out. I tried giving her some wind cover, and when Dounia finally lit up she took such a deep drag on her cigarette I thought she'd go up in smoke herself.

'What's your little game?'

'Meaning?'

'Oh, please! Don't take me for a complete airhead!'

'I simply gave my point of view!'

'You were spiteful!'

'No I wasn't! I didn't agree with your man, that's all... or isn't that allowed? Come off it, Dounia, he was talking bullshit! He was mixing everything up!'

'You do know he was responsible for handling the Ali Semsini affair? The kid who started firing on students in a Marseille lycée, d'you remember? About two years ago!'

'Yes, I remember.'

'Well then, stop talking to him like he's unqualified! He's an expert on the subject. What he sees are extremists, young people who've lost their way, some of whom, let me tell you, leave prison, hang with the wrong crowd and get a ticket for Afghanistan!'

'But what does the fight against terrorism have to do with excluding girls who wear the veil from school? And what's Ali Semsini got to do with you? You think you're some kind of role model for boys like him?'

'I don't claim to be a role model for anyone. But I thought you might make the effort to get to know Bernard! Instead, you did nothing but argue with him! I could have been listening to Maman!'

'Look, Dounia, your problem is you're after revenge! None of this has anything to do with me. Maman's Maman, and

I'm me.'

'I know. Okay, I shouldn't have said that... but please, make an effort? Be nice to him, for my sake. I'm really committed to him.'

'We've had no contact for ten years! And now you're wanting everything to happen too quickly! Next up, you'll be asking me to witness your wedding! You can't make me hit it off with him or to share his views!'

'I never said I wanted you to! But you could try not being rude. I was so looking forward to introducing Bernard to another member of my family...'

'Was I really so rude?'

'You were disrespectful. Listen, Mourad, I need to tell you something, I had a bit of a sensitive health issue last year, which left me sterile. I can no longer have children... It's something that's very painful for me to come to terms with, and it's affected me deeply. Nothing will ever grow inside my womb. But I have Bernard, he's here, he supports me, he loves me and takes care of me. If only for that, you owe it to the guy to give him a chance...'

Philip Morris smoke was wafting from her nostrils.

'I know it's stupid,' she added, inhaling again, 'but I often think Maman's won... because I can't stop thinking about her, about what she would have said or done. The thing is, a few years back, I fell pregnant, but it was an unwanted pregnancy and it was my body after all. I had an abortion, the timing was all wrong, I didn't want a kid, not like that... But today I can hear Maman's voice cackling in my ear: "You're being punished! You're paying for what you've done!"'

I put my hand on her shoulder while she crushed her cigarette with her shoe.

She gestured as if to say *Forget it, come on, let's talk about something else.*

Maybe she would adopt some East Asian children. Tartois would throw his energies into persuading Dounia to travel all the way to China for them, what with the compelling economic and geopolitical arguments.

Dounia started up again about going to see Big Baba.

'What time's your flight, Mourad?' she asked, tapping away at her Blackberry. And, when I told her, hey presto, 'Done!'

Having bought her ticket, she disappeared off to the Ladies, where she stayed for a while. Everyone was looking for her: the ambassador, the minister's principal private secretary and her Bernie-kins.

My sister's in love with her Bernard, it's glaringly obvious. Her vision may be blurred but I've got the eyes of a fighter pilot and I'm telling you he's a one-of-a-kind asshole. I wonder if the shrink she sees twice a week agrees with me but can't say so, given the duty of confidentiality.

What bothers me about men like Tartois is their sleazy generosity, their latent racism, their convictions wrapped up in carefully chosen vocabulary, and the deliberate confusion they sow. We'll see what they reap.

I hate how they're so persuaded that what they can teach you is worth more than everything you already know.

Tartois would be the kind of person to say to Babar:

'Sure, you wear patent moccasins and a bowtie, but have you taken a proper look at yourself in the mirror, my fat friend? You're an elephant! Nothing more! And as for that fat trunk you drag everywhere, weighing in at 100 kilos, don't tell me you haven't noticed it? Because it's the *only* thing we see! You're nothing but an elephant, you came into this world an elephant and as an elephant you'll croak it.'

The Fruit That Falls From The Tree

To streamline things for parents' evening, I had made an index card for each of my students, listing their strengths and weaknesses in two columns. Some of them warranted little in either column. These are the more 'transparent' students I fear I may have forgotten in two or three years' time.

As with every first occasion, I was freaked out.

While I sat there at my classroom desk, waiting for the first parents to arrive, I clipped two biros to my jacket pocket.

It was my tribute to Big Baba, the finest tribute I could pay him.

The parents of young Murugan Urvashi, from my Year 10 class, were the first to enter. I remembered Madame Laurent, one of the Maths teachers, remarking one day: 'I struggle to pronounce some of those Indian names, but let me tell you, their parents are always first in line for parents' evenings...'

Monsieur and Madame Urvashi smiled as they walked into the classroom, while Murugan, who was at least 15cm taller than his mother and father, trailed behind with his head down, looking ashamed, despite his outstanding grades. His embarrassment caught me off-guard.

As they listened attentively to me, I couldn't help noticing that his parents' heads bobbled from side to side with such striking regularity they could have been following a metronome. *Was this some kind of a tic?* What did I know? I didn't want them to think I was racist, so I pressed on.

I said something along the lines of: 'I'm pleased to tell you that Murugan has been getting top marks in French and is making pleasing progress, he's a very intelligent student!'

They carried on staring at me and smiling blankly.

Murugan broke his silence.

'Sir, my parents don't speak French very well, but they understand a little...'

I gave Monsieur and Madame Urvashi a silly thumbs up, which seemed to have the right effect because they laughed a little and looked relieved. Murugan translated a few snippets for them, and his parents appeared to be happy, they laughed again and were filled with pride. It was wonderful to behold. They thanked me warmly and shook my hand before leaving the room, satisfied.

My index cards, with the keywords written on them, were working well as prompts. Parents came and went, they were more or less involved in their child's progress, more or less shattered after their working day.

Sylvestre Douville's mother, with her freckled cheeks, was worried about her only son. 'He didn't have a complex about his ginger hair in Year 6! But now some of the black kids make fun of him in class. 'Mum,' he tells me, 'I want to be black, but have you ever seen a black kid with red hair?''

I pointed out to Madame Douville that Sylvestre was producing some excellent written work. He might not have many friends, but he possessed a lively imagination.

Monsieur Rahim, whose son Saïd was a model student, spoke to me in Arabic: 'If he causes any trouble, you hit him!

Agreed? Let him have it! Afterwards, tell me and I'll hit him again!'

Jonathan Krief's father came back into the classroom to give me a piece of his mind, 'I want my son to switch classes! This one is rubbish. And you're behind with the curriculum!' Then he scratched his neck and asked me: 'How old are you anyway? 21?'

Asma and Sarah Zerdad's mother was clasping her daughters warmly by the shoulder, one on either side. The resemblance was striking. All three had big black eyes with long eyelashes. Seeing them together brought back images from my childhood, images from before everything was broken.

Madame Zerdad could hardly believe her ears at my enthusiasm. She kissed her daughters' cheeks, stroked their hair and smiled brilliantly.

'If I only had Asmas and Sarahs in my classes, everything would be perfect! You should be very proud!'

'I am very, very proud of my children. Thanks be to God,' said Madame Zerdad, glancing again at the phrase '*exceeds expectations*' on both their report cards. 'Papa will jump for joy when we show him this!' she exclaimed, turning to Sarah.

Next, I heard some familiar beatboxing before Mehdi Mazouani appeared, his face still covered in bruises. He was staring at me as he made his way towards my desk.

'They really got you, didn't they?' I said.

'Whatevva, man.'

He turned around and, seeing as no one was following him, called out, 'Papa! Papaa! S'over here, innit!'

A squat stocky man with small dark eyes and thick, unruly eyebrows entered the classroom. His fingers were drumming on a small leather bag.

A cigarette was wedged behind his right ear, just like Mehdi the first time I'd seen him.

Monsieur Mazouani gave me a limp handshake and then pulled up a chair.

Mehdi insisted on standing despite me urging him to sit down with us.

''Low it man, s'cool, I'm not tired.'

The father kept blinking like a deer. He didn't bother looking at Mehdi's report card when I handed it over (admittedly, it was far from glorious). He was happy to fold it in four and stuff it inside his leather bag.

'Monsieur Mazouani, we need to have a serious talk about Mehdi's future. It would be a pity for him to ruin his chances. We should think about next year...'

'Look, M'sieur, I know what he's like, my boy. I'm used to him giving me a headache, aren't I? I'm in the tiling trade, see. They're always on the lookout for young kids in plastering, boilers, air-con, all that. They'll give them work, the bosses.'

'Maybe he'd like to do something else?'

'He can only screw things up! He smokes drugs! It's me who smashed his face in, isn't it? His mum's still blubbing! "You shouldn't hit him!" she says. Words are wasted on him, he never understands. He's not smart like his brothers and sisters, he's the last one, damaged goods. He's screwing up his life, you hear me. At 15, he's a man. In Tunisia, 15 means you're a man – no ifs, I'm telling you, no buts. He needs a job!'

So Mehdi had made that whole story up, from start to finish, about the gang at Maraîchers station. It sounded better than being beaten up by a dad who referred to you as 'damaged goods'.

Now I came to think about it, Big Baba had never raised

his hand against any of us. He settled for words, even when he was furious.

'In any case, school is compulsory until next year.'

'Even if I give him permission to leave?'

'Even so. We'll make an appointment with the careers' advisor,' I suggested, calculating that my first port of call should be the safeguarding officer. 'And that will enable us to discuss what the options might be for next year.... Does that sound okay, Mehdi...?'

Mehdi nodded unenthusiastically, but his eyes betrayed what he was really thinking: 'Like, do I even givva-shit?'

I had gathered up my belongings and Miloud had taken his clippers to my hair.

A proper cut from the old country, blédard-style.

'You don't know about these things!' he protested, when I suggested he remove the small bird's nest he'd left on top. 'You look good like that! It's 'fashun' – trust me, cuz.'

You've got to hand it to Mario. He'd made a special batch of rhubarb brioches for me to take back to Nice. Not only was he 100 percent reliable and clean-cut, but he showered us with small acts of kindness.

It was on the tip of my tongue to say, 'Mario, you're like a mother to me.'

Would he have taken it the right way?

Just as for my arrival, my dear cousin Miloud drove me to Roissy-Charles-de-Gaulle airport, and, just as for my arrival, I was enjoying the extra legroom in his Mercedes C-Class while he blasted out the raï.

In the plane, there were more safety instructions delivered by a ditzy air hostess.

Dounia was engrossed in her Blackberry, her thumb hovering above the keys as she read her e-mails.

'Don't worry, I've switched it to airplane mode.'

My neighbour, this time, was a retired man. He was fast asleep with his mouth wide open and his nose whistling a tune. The sideways view revealed a slender thread of dribble and, in his ear, a hearing aid tangled up in long white hairs. Each time I notice an old person's ears, I think, *Ears of that age must have heard so much nonsense in their time.*

It felt like an assignment for Scotland Yard.

Our plane landed at 4.45pm, but I'd told Maman I was arriving into Nice at 7pm. I hoped that would give me enough time to get to the hospital with Dounia, see Big Baba, make my way back to the airport with my suitcase and feign the expression of someone who'd just landed: fatigue, jetlag, all that.

'What if he's changed his mind? Maybe he doesn't want to see me anymore.'

'Stop talking rubbish.'

'I'm petrified.'

'Take it easy. Don't think about it too much. It'll be fine.'

'I hope so.'

'Dounia?'

'Yes?'

'How much d'you weigh?'

'What kind of a question is that?'

'Dunno. It's just you're so skinny.'

'There are some things you shouldn't ask a person! Like their age!'

'Okay... I didn't mean to get your back up, sorry.'

'You have the strangest ideas, sometimes...'

Dounia had picked like a sparrow at her meal tray before heading straight for the toilet afterwards.

Thinking back on it, she had gone to the toilet the day we ate lunch at café Flore too, and she'd stayed in there a while. At the time, I'd put it down to the raw meat.

Same thing at the Swedish embassy. *What's she doing in there?* I'd mused, *Power-napping?*

Does Dounia push her fingers down her throat?

It reminded me of those TV reports where vacant, emaciated, exhausted girls stare sadly at their plates, pushing a bit of tomato around with the tines of their fork.

Perhaps she despises herself? Perhaps she's ashamed of her body? Perhaps she doesn't see herself the way she really is? (Meaning skinny.)

So now I'm looking at Dounia and I'm picturing her throwing up.

The Finishing Line

I'm fascinated by athletes, their capacity to see something all the way through, to surpass themselves, to redefine their limits.

There's a whole ritual around big, televised athletics championships: the results table, the look in the eye of the athlete making a supreme effort, victory and close-up on the gold medal.

I feel nostalgic for the male comradery I used to share with Big Baba in front of the television set.

I can still see the face of Noureddine Morceli winning the 1500m final at the Olympic Games in Atlanta.

Big Baba wept that day. I swear. I'm sure I saw him crying, even if he claimed otherwise; flat denial, accompanied by loud sniffing.

'Have you taken leave of your senses? This is sinusitis!'

'Yeeeesss! Yeeeesss! Morceliiiiiii! Morceliiii!' screamed the Algerian commentator, who had no scruples about crying. 'Olympic gold for Algeria!!!! In three minutes and thirty-five point seven five seconds!'

The Moroccan, Hicham El Guerrouj, had been hotly tipped. He was in the leading pack when the poor man fell catastrophically on the final lap. They showed the scene in slow-motion several times on Canal Algeria. As well as the close-up on El Guerrouj collapsing in tears.

I'll never forget that moment. Noureddine Morceli looking incredulous as he caught his breath, the Algerian national anthem ringing out around the stadium, Big Baba's 'sinusitis,' and the flag that billowed on both their shoulders, the one in Atlanta and the other in our living room in Nice.

Dounia suggested we rent a car on our arrival at the airport.

With Europcar, you rent a lot more than a car.

So what does that mean, apart from the keys and a full tank?

'All I've got left is a three-door Twingo,' explained the rental assistant. 'Will that do?'

'I leave that to your better judgement!' said Dounia.

Wow! I reckoned it was the first time I'd heard someone say the words 'I leave that to your better judgement!' in real life.

It was only a ten-kilometre drive to the hospital.

Dounia drove nervously, clinging to the steering wheel with her bony hands, so the car jolted, and the back of my head kept banging against the headrest.

'I haven't driven in yonks! I always take taxis in Paris!'

As we turned the bend on a road overlooking the city, we glimpsed the Mediterranean.

I thought about Mehdi Mazouani and reflected that growing up beside the sea is a stroke of luck.

I pictured my mother busily preparing a gargantuan dinner. The table would be heaving with food by now, including the following as a minimum spread: matlou flatbreads, avocado milkshakes, grilled peppers, salad, fried aubergines, lamb tajine with prunes and almonds, spit-roasted saffron chicken and sautéed potatoes.

'You've eaten nothing, my son!' Maman would complain,

after watching me stuff my face to the point of clogging my arteries. 'What's the matter? Are you sick? Perhaps you're running a fever?'

Mina would have cleaned the house like a fanatic, disinfecting the toilets and mopping everywhere in sight. The smell of bleach and lemon-scented Saint-Marc all-surface cleaner would tickle my nostrils as I crossed the threshold.

The children would have grown, and they'd jump all over me shouting: 'Tonton! Tonton! You're back!'

I'd feel emotional as I glanced at our certificates framed with pride by Big Baba on the living room wall.

I've missed home.

Dounia would be on her own in her small Niçois apartment, chain-smoking on the balcony, filling her empty belly with smoke while checking her e-mails and waiting on the phone-call from Tartois, who'd be busy with his cronies in the National Assembly.

'I feel like I'm hallucinating,' Dounia remarked, as we walked into the neuro rehab unit, 'and my knees have gone all wobbly.'

Big Baba had his back to us. He was facing the window and watching the day's first drops of rain. He had always loved the rain and used to go outside into his garden just to breathe in the smell of damp earth, every time it rained.

The shutters were half-closed, and we could just make out that his roommate was an elderly Indian gentleman who sat stock-still, staring at us.

Big Baba's shoulders looked hunched in his hospital gown, and his temples seemed to have turned even whiter.

Dounia put both hands to her mouth, as if to stifle a cry; her eyes brimmed with tears, reminding me of a river after an unexpected flood.

'Papa!' I called out.

He turned around, slowly, and his wheelchair squeaked on the green linoleum floor. I went over to kiss him on his cheeks and forehead.

'How are you, my boy?!' he asked softly.

Then, pointing to a leaflet on his bedside table, he added: 'I was waiting for you to read that to me in a journalist's voice...'

Hiding behind me, Dounia put her hand on his shoulder. She was trembling all over and her cheeks were covered in the salt from her tears, like a sadness archived inside her for more than ten years.

It took a few seconds before Big Baba finally recognised her. His expression was one of joy and incomprehension, just like Noureddine Morceli in 1996, at the finishing line.

His face puckered and he began to cry, putting aside his emotional reserve, releasing his innermost feelings and breaking with his own commandment: *Men Don't Cry*. His brow was furrowed as he wept into his daughter's chest, his face against her breastbone. Sickness, death and the solemnity of life make us temporarily forget our old resentments.

A few minutes later, Big Baba was staring obsessively at his neighbour's bedside table, as he pointed out a small statue to us.

'Tell him to remove it! I want him to remove it!'

The elderly Indian gentleman began to scowl and shout as he grabbed his statue and clutched it to his chest.

'Is Ganesh! Not touch! Is Ganesh!'

'Just wait for him to doze off,' Big Baba told Dounia. 'I'm going to take that cursed statue of his and I'm going to smash it against the wall!'

'Don't work yourself up, Papa. Perhaps he needs it...' Dounia murmured, stroking his wrist.

Big Baba shook his head.

'What does he need a statue for, eh? His elephant will stop the angels from visiting my room! That's why he's keeping his eyes wide open, and he's burst all his blood vessels as a result, just look at him! He hasn't dared sleep in two days because he knows I'm going to smash that stupid statue of his!'

The Indian gentleman's eyes bulged as he continued to cradle his Ganesh close to his heart.

'Haaaaaaaaa! Is Ganesh! Is Ganesh! Not touch!' he insisted, while bobbling his head from right to left with uncanny regularity. Shades of the parents of young Murugan Urvashi a few days earlier.

The commotion had rallied the entire care team.

'Well, good afternoon, everybody...' said a young nurse who had entered the room and was standing, hand on hip. 'Goodness me! What seems to be the matter, Monsieur Chennoun?!'

'*He* started it! The Hindu! He's the one who started it!'

'Excuse me! Our friend has a name, doesn't he? Monsieur Ishana may not speak much French, but he understands it perfectly well!'

The elderly Indian gentleman's eyes bulged further on hearing his name.

'I don't want to know his name! I'm not in the least bit interested in his name!'

'Why are you arguing like this?! We thought you'd enjoy having a roommate, making a new friend!'

'I don't need a friend!'

The Indian gentleman kissed his statue of Ganesh while watching my father, his eyes injected with blood.

'Did you see that, Mourad? Eh? You saw that! He did it on purpose! Devil's accomplice! He's provoking me! You wait until I start walking again! I'll skin you alive!'

Big Baba was like a child.

'I didn't realise it had come to this!' Dounia confided in me. She looked overwhelmed but happy to see Big Baba again.

'Ah, here you are! You've returned! I can die in peace!'

Dounia stroked Big Baba's lifeless arm, unable to offer a reply except to whisper: 'I'm sorry, Papa...'

The Final Destination

A fresh rain began to fall. That reassuring smell of damp earth and humidity, combined with an astonishing silence.

The water fell on our heads, it weighed down the branches of the olive trees and carried off the refuse from the town in rivulets.

When I turned around, there, a few metres behind Mina, my mother, and my aunts, I could see Dounia drying her tears in her scarf. Her over-long djellaba trailing in the mud. My mother held out her hand and drew her eldest daughter close. Yes, sickness, death and the solemnity of life make us temporarily forget our old resentments.

On our arrival, one of Big Baba's sisters was crying so hard she ended up biting her own hand.

'You're bringing him back to us in a box!' she gasped, between sobs. 'You're returning him to us laid out in a box.'

If we hadn't held her back, she'd have thrown herself on top of the coffin.

The women didn't follow us for the committal but swept into the house, where I thought I could glimpse 1000 silhouettes comforting one another.

As for the men, we made our way solemnly towards the cemetery. At the head of the cortège, the coffin carried by the honourable volunteers.

We followed.

And we will follow next. Yes, the same thought preoccupies us all: 'The cemetery is our final destination.'

The clouds were swelling before our eyes, in infinite hues of grey. I had never seen the Algerian sky outside of summertime before.

A street hawker was pushing his wooden cart arrayed with the sardines he had caught that morning at Beni Saf. On encountering our procession, he stopped running for a few metres as a sign of respect.

There were at least 200 mourners in the cortège, all walking with their heads down, as if their necks had crumpled under the weight of the sky.

You wouldn't think so but clouds weigh tonnes.

Naturally, I was inspecting everyone's shoes, and if you counted them by unit rather than pairs, that made for at least 400. Once a cobbler's son, always a cobbler's son.

'We belong to Allah and to Him shall we return,' people kept saying to me. It didn't matter that I didn't recognise who half of them were. At the mosque in Nice, on the eve of our departure, plenty of men I'd never met before came to join me in praying over Big Baba, and so they became my brothers. I who had grown up with none.

Big Baba's corpse in the coffin was a reminder to us all, for me as his son, just as it was for the men closing the ranks of the funeral prayer. There was no escaping that one day it would be our turn to lie in a coffin.

In the funeral parlour, when I had kissed his icy forehead, I reflected that Big Baba was merely ahead of the rest of us in leaving the prison of this world, and that one day we would be reunited, if God wills it.

His face seemed luminous to me. After the ritual washing, he had been anointed with musk while rose petals had been scattered in his coffin. Wrapped in his shroud, he looked like a prince.

I kept thinking that, at any second, I might turn around and see him in the crowd, standing by the grave of the dead person, a dead person who wasn't him but someone else, whose loss would make us feel sad, and nothing more. In any event, it wouldn't hurt so much.

A coronary thrombosis, in the middle of the night, towards 3am. A male nurse delivering the news over the telephone, my tears streaming down the touch-sensitive screen, a flood of tears, and that question I couldn't help asking myself: 'Why don't men cry?'

He left without giving me a chance to ask him.

I received messages of condolence from Liliane, Miloud and even Hélène. But what was I meant to do with other people's compassion? It seemed pointless to me.

If I had to say one last thing about my father, I would do so in a journalist's voice: *Big Baba may have been illiterate, but he knew how to read me better than anyone.*

From now on, we have got to start again from zero.

But it's always the same old refrain: no one ever starts again from zero, not even the Arabs who invented it, as Big Baba used to say.

Acknowledgements

The translator would like to thank:

Bel Parker, for her invaluable and inspired assistance at an early stage of the manuscript, especially with the representation of Algerian Arabic in English, her suggestion to move the Tsunami chapter, and for helping to voice Cindy in chapter 11. Also, for her energetic eye and brilliant wit.

Rohan Ayinde for his wisdom in advising on the voice of Mehdi Mazouani in freestyle dialogue, so that distilling some of the rhythm and vibrancy and texture of French backslang spoken by a young man of Algerian heritage – and reimagining it riffing off multiethnic urban English – holds true as an act affection.

Bibi Bakare-Yusuf for believing passionately in this book's journey into the English language for readers from Abuja to Brixton and far beyond.

Mathias Rambaud and Louise Cambau for generously facilitating a short stay at the Institut Français in London to finish the first draft of this translation – gifting me with no worldly responsibilities and only a guinea pig for company.

Steve Cook, Dr David Swinburne and Katharine McMahon at the Royal Literary Fund, and Will Forrester at English PEN – for their luminous support.

And, finally, Faïza and Rebecca Carter for the vibrant odyssey of our friendship over the years, and which keeps nourishing us.

Support *Men Don't Cry*

We hope you enjoyed reading this book. It was brought to you by Cassava Republic Press, an award-winning independent publisher based in Abuja and London. If you think more people should read this book, here's how you can help:

Recommend it. Don't keep the enjoyment of this book to yourself; tell everyone you know. Spread the word to your friends and family.

Review, review review. Your opinion is powerful and a positive review from you can generate new sales. Spare a minute to leave a short review on Amazon, GoodReads, Wordery, our website and other book buying sites.

Join the conversation. Hearing somebody you trust talk about a book with passion and excitement is one of the most powerful ways to get people to engage with it. If you like this book, talk about it, Facebook it, Tweet it, Blog it, Instagram it. Take pictures of the book and quote or highlight from your favourite passage. You could even add a link so others know where to purchase the book from.

Buy the book as gifts for others. Buying a gift is a regular activity for most of us – birthdays, anniversaries, holidays, special days or just a nice present for a loved one for no reason... If you love this book and you think it might resonate with others, then please buy extra copies!

Get your local bookshop or library to stock it. Sometimes bookshops and libraries only order books that they have heard about. If you loved this book, why not ask your librarian or bookshop to order it in. If enough people request a title, the bookshop or library will take note and will order a few copies for their shelves.

Recommend a book to your book club. Persuade your book club to read this book and discuss what you enjoy about the book in the company of others. This is a wonderful way to share what you like and help to boost the sales and popularity of this book. You can also join our online book club on Facebook at Afri-Lit Club to discuss books by other African writers.

Attend a book reading. There are lots of opportunities to hear writers talk about their work. Support them by attending their book events. Get your friends, colleagues and families to a reading and show an author your support.

Thank you!

Transforming a manuscript into the book you are now reading is a team effort. Cassava Republic Press would like to thank everyone who helped in the production of *Men Don't Cry*:

Editorial
Bibi Bakare-Yusuf
Layla Mohamed

Design & Production
Tobi Ajiboye
Jamie Keenan

Sales & Marketing
Kofo Okunola
Niki Igbaroola

Publicity
Fiona Brownlee